oh my goth

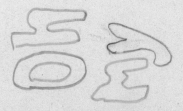

oh my goth
gena showalter

POCKET BOOKS   MTV BOOKS

New York   London   Toronto   Sydney

POCKET BOOKS, a division of Simon & Schuster, Inc.
1230 Avenue of the Americas, New York, NY 10020

ISBN-13: 978-1-4165-2474-8
ISBN-13:   1-4165-2474-6

This MTV Books/Pocket Books trade paperback edition July 2006

10 9 8 7 6 5 4 3 2 1

For information regarding special discounts for bulk purchases,
please contact Simon & Schuster Special Sales at 1-800-456-6798
or business@simonandschuster.com.

To the ladies who helped me every step of the way: Jill Monroe, Kelli McBride, Sheila Fields, Donnell Epperson, Amanda McCabe, Betty Sanders, Nancy Cochran, Deidre Knight, Lauren McKenna, and Megan McKeever.

To Samantha Jenkins, Elaine Spencer and Julie Ramsey. A trinity of superpowers and fun.

To the wonderful girls who told me about their high school experience because I couldn't remember my own. Listen to Auntie Gena—don't do the things you know you shouldn't do. But if you screw up, go ahead and e-mail me the story.

And to The Max, my high school sweetheart, who is still with me today.

oh my goth

chapter one

When people look at me, they automatically assume I'm dark and weird. Why can't they see the truth? I'm just a girl, trying to find my place in the world.
From the journal of Jade Leigh

god, I hate school.

I'm sitting in trig, listening (not really) to Mr. Parton drone on and on about angles and measurements. As if I care. As if I'll ever use that stuff outside of this classroom.

Honestly, I'd rather be anywhere else. Even home, where my dad begins almost every conversation with, "You should lose the black clothes and wear something with color." Puh-lease. Like I *want* to look like every Barbie clone in Hell

High, a.k.a. Oklahoma's insignificant Haloway High School. Ironically, Dad doesn't appreciate the bright blue streaks in my originally blond/now-dyed-black hair. Go figure. That's *color*, right?

With my elbows resting on my desktop, I dropped my forehead into my upraised palms and closed my eyes. Mr. Parton continued to blah, blah, blah (or, as he'd tell you, talk), and his superior, I-know-the-answers-therefore-I-am-God voice grated against my nerves.

Was I surprised? No. He *always* talked to us like that, as if we were dumb for not already knowing how to work math equations we'd never encountered before. He even got mad when we asked questions—God forbid we actually learn, right?—and generally treated us like total dumbwits.

Fifteen minutes, thirty-seven seconds before bell. Translation: fifteen minutes, thirty-seven seconds of me wishing for an apocalyptic destruction of the universe so my misery would end.

What had I done to deserve this kind of torture? Talk back to my dad? Who didn't? Ditch a few classes? Show me one person who hasn't. Pierce my nose? Well . . .

"If Miss Leigh will give me the honor of her attention," Mr. Parton snapped, "I'll explain the relation between sins and chords."

I didn't glance up, didn't want to encourage him. Really, when would this end?

"Are you paying attention, Miss Leigh, or are you praying you never come into contact with a wooden stake?"

Several students chuckled.

I still didn't bother looking up, but I *did* react to his taunt. "No, I'm not," I gritted out. I think the man enjoyed making fun of me more than he liked teaching. Not a single day passed without a snide comment from him: Why don't you do everyone a favor and stay home tomorrow, Miss Leigh? You're the reason I need ulcer medication, Miss Leigh. Your poor father, he must need a lot of therapy, huh, Miss Leigh. I'd heard it all. "FYI," I added, "your comment doesn't make you fright, Mr. Parton."

"Fright." Avery Richards snorted. "That's such a dumb word."

"Just say *cool* like the rest of us," someone else said.

I felt my cheeks heat with embarrassment—and hated myself for letting them see any hint of upset.

Mr. Parton tapped his foot impatiently. "Mind sharing with us what you were doing that's more important than listening to what I have to say? If anyone in this classroom needs to learn, it's you."

Okay. Now I'm officially pissed. "If you must know, I'm thinking of less painful ways to kill myself than from your lesson. *Kevin.*"

My classmates erupted into laughter, and I heard the shuffle of their seats as they turned to glance at me. They may not like me, but they always found my irreverence amusing.

Mr. Parton glared. "You will address me as 'Mr. Parton' or not address me at all. You do *not* call me by my first name. Ever. I don't want someone like you even thinking it."

How's this for a math equation: the wooden stake comment plus the someone-like-you comment equals a ready-to-throw-down Jade Leigh. His words assured one thing: I would not allow myself to back down now.

"Is it okay, then, if I call you Kevie?" I said. I'm Goth; that doesn't make me a vampire. If I were, I would have drained Mr. Parton a long time ago.

Honestly, I'm not evil. I liked to dabble in the magical arts (upon occasion), yes, and I dressed to set myself apart from the ultratraditional norm. There's nothing wrong with expressing my individuality.

"There *will* be a quiz on this information," he growled. "While I'm happy to give you an F, I'll be even happier to give you detention if you don't start paying attention."

He expected me to shake with fear over the thought of detention. If he'd said something about "extreme makeover" or "an hour of shopping with the Barbie clones" . . . maybe. But an hour alone with my thoughts?

Yeah, I'm quaking.

Just keep your mouth shut, Jade, my common sense piped in. Ignore him. *You can't afford to be in trouble again.* I looked up at last, facing him, determined (finally) to remain silent and end our battle. He wouldn't get in trouble for it, but I would. Yet, when my gaze locked with his, his too-thin lips curled in a smug smile and his green eyes glowed with triumph—as if he'd already won.

"That's what I thought," he said, his voice as smug as his grin.

"Detention sounds like fun," I found myself saying, all sense of preservation annihilated by his premature smugness. "Sign me up. I can hardly wait to start."

His eyes narrowed to tiny slits, and his face darkened to an angry red, clashing with his white button-up shirt (no wrinkles) and brown dress slacks (again, no wrinkles). So neat. So tidy.

At one time, I bet he'd been military.

That's probably why he'd taken an instant dislike to me at the beginning of the school year. Military men, like my dad, liked things precise, nothing out of place. I usually wore a black vinyl shirt lined with cobweb lace, fishnet gloves, and ripped jeans. Or, like today, a frayed black mini and black Victorian corset. *Soooo* not "precise" and completely out of place. My black lip liner and nose ring probably didn't help.

What do you think he'd do if he saw the symbol of infinity tattooed around my navel?

"You want detention so badly I'll sign you up for the entire week." He crossed his arms over his chest, obviously expecting me to rush out an apology. "How would you like that?"

When would he learn I wasn't like the other kids at this school?

"Mr. Parton," I said, studying my metallic blue nail polish

as if I hadn't a care in the world. Inside, though, I hadn't forgotten that I stood on the edge of a jagged cliff, trouble waiting for me if I fell. But I couldn't seem to help myself; I despised this man too much. "Do you mind getting back to your lecture, so I can get back to my nap?"

Another round of laughter erupted.

"That's it!" Scowl deepening, he pounded toward me and slapped his hand against my desk, causing the metal legs to vibrate. If he didn't learn to control his stress level, he'd burst a vessel in his forehead. "You've been nothing but a nuisance for three weeks. You have the worst grades in the class—in *all* your classes, actually. I checked."

My back straightened, and my shoulders squared. How dare this "role model" discuss my grades with the entire class. "I have an A in creative writing," I informed him staunchly.

"Well, good for you." The sarcastic edge in his voice grated against my every nerve. "You know how to write in your native language. Woohoo. Let's all give Miss Leigh a round of applause."

More laughter (no longer in my favor), followed by the sound of enthusiastic hand clapping and whistling. *Traitors!* I should have expected nothing less.

My eyes narrowed, and I think Mr. Parton realized I was about to rip into him. He slapped my desk again. "We're done with this conversation. I've had enough of you, and I want you out." He jerked a finger toward the door. "Get out of my classroom. Go straight to the principal's office. Do not talk to anyone. Do not stop in the bathroom."

What, should I collect two hundred dollars if I passed Go?

Tomblike silence claimed the room as I bent to retrieve my books and red velvet purse from the floor. "Don't you need to write me a note or something?" I said, purposefully keeping my tone light. No way I'd give him the "please let me stay" reaction he craved.

His nostrils flared before he stomped to his desk, scribbled something on a piece of paper, and thudded back to me. He smacked that sheet into my outstretched palm. "Out!"

"Thanks," I said, proud of myself. I hadn't backed down, hadn't let him intimidate me. As my mom once said, "If you don't stand up for yourself, Jade sweetie, no one else will. Be strong. Be brave. Be *you*."

She'd uttered those words right before she died.

Two years ago, a distracted driver had slammed into our car, propelling us into the one in front of us. I'd been fifteen at the time, and she had been teaching me how to drive. I lost my mom that day, as well as the illusion of immortality. I had almost died myself and still bore the scars on my abdomen, so I understood how short life could be. I would not allow a man like Mr. Parton to ruin a single day of mine.

I may only be seventeen years old, but that doesn't mean I'm stupid. That doesn't mean I'm powerless. Mr. Parton enjoys taking his frustrations out on his class. He spills coffee on his shirt, we get a quiz. He locks his keys in his car, we get ten pages of homework.

What's more, I (obviously) can't stand the way he talks to me, as if I'm less of a person than he is because I'm younger, because I dress differently. Should I be punished for not liking math (and sucking at it)? Should I be punished for dabbling in what others considered the darker side of life?

"Pick up the pace," he told me irritably. "The sooner you're gone, the sooner the rest of the class can enjoy the lesson."

I pushed to my feet and adjusted the bag over my shoulder. "I don't think you have to worry about anyone enjoying it."

The comment earned several snickers.

His teeth bared in a scowl, and he took a menacing step toward me. The man looked ready to snap—my neck, that is. A little tremble worked through me, but I quickly squashed it. If I showed any weakness, he would only use it against me in our next skirmish.

And there would be another one. There always was.

I remained in place, taking comfort in the fact that Mr. Parton had to look up at me. I'm taller than he is by several inches—and I'm only five foot seven. I'd bet my college savings he suffers from a Napoleon complex.

See, I pay attention in some of my classes.

"You come back in here and you'll regret it. Do you understand me?"

"That's something I already knew, Kev, what with you and your lecturing . . ." Without waiting for his reply, I gave him a finger wave and headed for the door. I knew everyone was watching me leave; I felt the heat of their gazes boring into my back. In case you're wondering, yes, this has happened to me many times before.

"Freak," someone muttered as I passed.

Mr. Parton smirked, not saying a word in rebuke. My cheeks again burned a bright red; my stomach clenched. I don't want to be one of the crowd, a clone like the rest of them, but I *do* want to be respected. I want to be accepted for who I am. No one enjoys being called horrible names.

"Moron."

"Loo-ser," I heard Mercedes Turner say. Beautiful, wealthy, utterly popular Mercedes Turner. She glanced up from her Sidekick, probably e-mailing one of her clone friends about me, and smirked. I hate, hate, *hate* her.

The only thing we have in common is the fact that we both only have one parent. Wait. That's not true. We have two things in common. She hates me as much as I hate her. Mortal enemies, that was us.

With her pale hair, blue eyes, perfect makeup and perfect clothes, she's Hell High's It girl. Every girl wants to be her (except me—gag!), and every boy wants to date her. I know for a fact that every boy wants to date her because she's stolen the ones *I've* wanted. The moment a boy shows any interest in me, Mercedes suddenly has to have him. She's determined to ruin my life, and I don't know why.

Unless you count the time I introduced her face to my fists. Over and over again.

"The world is a better place without her mom," she'd

mumbled to her friends only a few days after my mom's funeral. She hadn't meant for me to hear, but I had and I'd exploded into action, hitting and kicking her with every ounce of my strength, every ounce of rage and impotence I'd felt at being unable to save my mother. My friends had had to pull me off of her.

Yes, I have friends here at school. Does it shock you to hear some people actually like me? Well, it shouldn't. They're outcasts like me. I hang with Erica, Linnie (short for Linda), and Robb. We eat lunch together every day and sometimes party after school. They're a lot like me, my friends. They love the joy of expression. They hate conformity. Hate hypocrisy. Hate the rigidness of what's supposedly "proper."

More importantly, they hate the Barbies. I could have used their moral support right now.

When I stood in the hall, the door closed tight behind me, I leaned against the cool red brick. I drew in a breath. Sweet escape. Alone at last, the burn in my cheeks began to fade. I glanced over the note Mr. Parton had written. The handwriting was almost unreadable, but I was able to make out "disrupt" and "no longer tolerate" and "expel."

I should be so lucky.

No. I sighed. Not true. Actually, I couldn't afford to be expelled. My grades weren't the best, but I was passing. If I were expelled, I would be given zeros for the missed work, and I would fail. If I failed, I wouldn't graduate and couldn't, at last, pursue my dream.

I want to be a writer.

Stupid, huh? I'd have better luck becoming a witch. My dad says only, like, one percent of writers actually get published. (When I told him my dream, he looked up the statistics on the Internet, hoping to talk some sense into me.) I love to write, though, and have countless notebooks and journals filled with my stories, my thoughts.

Oh, the magic . . . the possibilities . . . the total lack of limitation I find within those pages. On paper, I can do impossible things. I can find acceptance for who I am—acceptance that always eludes me in real life.

With another sigh, I pushed down the hall. Posters that read VOTE FOR MERCEDES littered the walls. They even had Mercedes's smiling, perfect picture. She wants to be student body president. The only way I'll vote for her is if a steaming pile of dog shit is my only other choice. And even then it's iffy. If I had a marker, I would have given her pictures fangs and horns.

Well, maybe not, I decided after a moment's thought. That would have insulted the devil.

Thankfully the hallways were devoid of students, so I didn't have to deal with anyone. That would change in about five minutes when everyone rushed to their next class. I quickened my step, the loud *clump-clump* of my boots echoing. When I reached the principal's office, I waved to the secretaries. They rolled their eyes.

"Jade, Jade, Jade." Cher, my favorite, tsked under her

tongue. Yes, that's her name, and yes, we're on a first-name basis. She has curly red hair, round cheeks, countless freckles, and a plump figure.

What I liked best about her, though, was that she always wore a fancy dress and didn't care what everyone else thought. No matter the occasion, she was dressed for prom. Today she wore an emerald green puffy . . . thing with ruffles down the center.

"I'll let Ms. Hamilton know you're here," she said, picking up the phone. "Have a seat."

The lobby was big, separated from the offices by a long yellow counter. There were three desks and a few scattered chairs. Computers, fax machines, phones that rang constantly. The walls were covered with red-and-black banners, our school colors. HOME OF THE FIGHTING STALLIONS they read. The jocks loved to refer to themselves as stallions—fighting, bucking, wild. Didn't matter.

They were a herd of idiots, in my opinion.

I turned toward the noncushioned seats in front of Ms. Hamilton's office. Ms. Hamilton purposefully made them as uncomfortable as possible, a subtle punishment meant to keep us away. One of the chairs was already occupied—by a boy I didn't recognize. A, uh, hot boy. A *really* hot boy.

The sight of him caught me off guard, and I blinked. Gulped. Stilled. I didn't mean to, but I stared at him, my breath caught in my throat. He had dark, messy hair, a square face, and heavy-lidded blue eyes that did strange things to my stomach.

Red alert!

His shoulders were wide and his gray T-shirt hugged his biceps. Obviously he worked out. A lot. Did he play basketball? Probably. Football? Most likely. The thought should have lessened his total hottiness because the jocks never tired of harassing me and my friends, calling us freaks and psychos. But it didn't.

I knew I should turn away, but couldn't.

The longer I stood here staring at him, the more stupid I probably looked. *Sit down, you idiot, and play it fright. Play it fright!* I forced my feet to move, one scuffed boot in front of the other.

"Hey," I said, easing into the seat across from him. Then I pressed my lips together. I shouldn't have said anything. He'd probably ignore me. He'd probably act like—

"Hey," he said, his voice deep, a little husky. He leaned back in the chair, untouchable. Detached from me and the rest of the world.

A moment passed before I realized he'd spoken. To me. He'd actually spoken to me. I relaxed against the seat. His gaze roved over me, slowly, taking me in inch by inch, and I experienced another flash of panic. Was my hair a mess? Was my skirt zipped? I gripped the hem of said skirt to keep from reaching up and checking. The silver chains circling my wrists dug into my thigh.

He gave me a mysterious half smile.

That grin made my palms sweat and my skin feel hot. I

didn't date—and not by my own choosing (hello, I'm a normal girl), but because the boys here never asked me out. Besides, I wasn't one hundred percent comfortable around boys. As I said, the ones I crushed on tended to fall for girls like Mercedes: perfect, blond, and disgustingly perky. Not that I'm crushing on this guy. Really.

"You, uh, new here?" I asked.

"Yeah. First day."

"Well, you're lucky you missed lunch. The food here sucks."

"Every school cafeteria is the same." As he spoke, he stretched out his jean-clad legs—his very long jean-clad legs. "Bad."

Covertly I looked him over, but I didn't see any piercings or tattoos, two things that would have placed him on my level. I frowned with disappointment. "What's your name?" I found myself asking.

"Clarik."

"Fright name." I paused. "That means I like it. I'm, uh, Jade."

"Thanks." He gave me another of those mysterious grins, this one even slower, more lethal. "Jade—pretty name."

"Thank you." My gaze traveled to the piece of paper folded in his hand. "That your schedule?"

"Yeah."

A boy of few words. I kind of liked that.

The bell rang, and the halls behind us jammed with students. I didn't have to turn and look out the glass wall to know. Their footsteps echoed in my ears, blending with the sound of slamming lockers and laughing chatter. Even the air changed, thickening with the scent of multiple perfumes and colognes.

"Who'd you get?" I asked, having to speak louder to be heard.

He read the paper. "Harper, Norfield, Reynolds, Parton, Frandemier, and Carroll."

Did we have Norfield and Parton at the same time? If so, I'd be happy to tutor him after school and bring him up to speed. Totally from the goodness of my heart, I assure you. I'm giving that way. A constant do-gooder. Really, I deserve a humanitarian award. A plaque at the very least.

Clarik sat up and leaned toward me, anchoring his elbows on his knees. He pinned me with an intense gaze. "I overslept and missed most of the day, so haven't gotten to meet any of them. Any words of advice for me?"

I didn't have to think about it. "Yeah. Get out of Parton's class."

He chuckled, and the husky sound of it washed over me. "An asshole, is he?"

"You have no—"

"Clarik," Cher called. "Your guide is here."

Immediately he stood and turned toward the girl now filling the entrance. I looked, too. When I saw her, I ground my teeth together. My nails dug into my fishnets. Mercedes. Of course. I should have known she'd arrive the moment the words "he's hot" passed through my mind. In her short pink skirt and white tank, she was as beautiful as ever. Her blond hair floated around her delicate shoulders.

My gaze flicked back to Clarik, who seemed riveted by the sight of her. Typical. And disappointing.

"You're Clarik?" she asked in surprise. She blushed prettily and ran her bottom lip between her teeth, the picture of innocence and sweetness. She even smiled shyly.

Talk about false advertising. Mercedes wasn't shy, wasn't innocent, and she sure as hell wasn't sweet.

Clarik cleared his throat. "Yep, that's me." He glanced down at me for the briefest of seconds. With dismissal? Or—and this was probably just wistful thinking on my part—regret? "Nice to meet you, Jade."

"Yeah," I gritted out. "You, too."

Mercedes finally noticed me and scowled. "Come on," she said to Clarik. She actually strolled to him, grabbed his arm, and tugged him beside her. "We need to get you out of this office before you're contaminated by the trash. I'll show you to your class."

They were off, the sound of Mercedes's chattering voice fading.

I gripped the edge of my seat to keep from sprinting after her and reintroducing her face to my fists. At this very second she was probably telling Clarik he shouldn't associate with me, that I was a horrible person, blah, blah, blah. I shouldn't care.

I'd just met him, and he meant nothing to me. But I couldn't stop sparks of anger from spreading through my veins.

Tomorrow Clarik would see me in the hall and probably turn the other way. He'd act like he had never met me, and call me a freak behind my back. Mercedes would smile smugly, like she always did.

I'd have to pretend it didn't bother me, like *I* always did. I would never—never!—let Mercedes know she hurt me. Like Mr. Parton, she'd use any perceived weakness against me for eternity.

Suddenly the principal's door burst open, claiming my attention. I shoved my enemy and her new (hot) target out of my mind. They weren't important. Right? Right. Wait, one last thought about Mercedes. What a bitch! Okay, now I was done.

My friend Linnie sailed out of the office, her jet-black hair in spikes around her head. She wore a flowing black dress, black hose, and heels. Her silver eyebrow ring glinted in the light.

Surprised to see her, I jolted to my feet. She spotted me, grinned, and skidded to a halt.

"What happened?" I asked. "Why are you here?"

"Hammy's in a wicked bad mood," she said loudly, not caring who heard. "Hammy" is what we call Principal Hamilton. Rarely to her face, though. "She gave me two days' vacation. Come to my house later. I'm having a party to celebrate."

Two days. Crap. What would *I* get if Linnie, who wasn't nearly as troublesome as me, got two days? Linnie didn't mind the expulsion, I knew, because she had money. Well, her parents had money and she had it by association. She didn't have to ever work, didn't have to attend college if she didn't want. To her, expulsion *was* a vacation.

"What'd you do?" I asked.

She opened her mouth to answer, but Ms. Hamilton appeared in the doorway and said, "Get in here, Leigh."

My heart skipped a traitorous beat.

Linnie's brows arched. "Told you," she said. "You're in for a world of hurt, my friend, and not in a good way. Enjoy."

chapter two

There are times I wish I were invisible.
Which is silly, since I do everything I can
to stand out.

as I trudged past, I handed Hammy the note Mr. Parton had written.

It would have done no good to "lose" the note before reaching the office. Mr. Parton would tattle on me (the big crybaby), and then I'd be in more trouble.

Was it possible to be in any more trouble, though?

My stomach twisted as I claimed the chair directly in front of the desk and carefully placed my bag at my ankles. I inhaled slowly, taking in the scent of lemon furniture polish and . . . vanilla? It was too sweet a scent for such a SIM-like lady.

Not yet wanting to face her, I looked around the small, cramped office. Books were scattered in every direction and antidrug posters covered the walls. A thin wooden table stretched against the far wall, folders piled along the edges. Papers spilled from the sides.

As she glanced over the note, Hammy plopped into her seat. When she'd read every word, she propped her elbows on the desk surface and stared over at me without expression. I tamped down the urge to squirm in my seat.

I'm not sure if I like Ms. Hamilton, and I don't know why. I mean, she never yells at students; instead, she uses a voice as monotone as a computer animation. There just doesn't seem to be any real personality to her. She's very plain and *very* old. I mean, she's like thirty-five or forty with mousy brown hair, brown eyes, and thin lips. She's the perfect candidate for *Make Your Teen Obey* magazine.

"You and Mr. Parton clashed again, did you?" she said without giving any hint to her thoughts. But then, she never gave any hint to her thoughts.

I shrugged, hoping I appeared nonchalant. "That's what the note says, isn't it?"

"I don't care what the note says. I want to hear what happened from you."

Right. I knew what that meant. She wanted me to admit I was wrong, that I'd overreacted. Well, I wouldn't and I hadn't. "He called me a vampire. I told him he sucked at teaching. I shouldn't be in trouble for that. I should be commended for telling the truth."

She pinched the bridge of her nose and shook her head. "Do you realize that every time you and Mr. Parton fight, you disrupt the entire class? You infringe on everyone else's right to learn."

Okay, so, score one for Hammy. "I know," I said softly, prickles of guilt weaving with my upset. "He provokes me. Doesn't that count for something?"

"No."

My eyes narrowed. "So it's okay for him to disrupt the class, but not me?"

"I didn't say that." She sighed.

"*He's* the adult. He should know better."

"Enough." She slapped her hand against the desk, a perfect mimic of Mr. Parton. Such a display of anger from her surprised me. "You've been in here six times already and the school year has barely begun. I've had you write essays. That didn't work. I've given you detention. That didn't work. What do you think I should try this time, Jade?"

Here it was. The old "you decide your punishment." My dad liked to utilize this technique, as well. I didn't mind telling Hammy what I always told him. "Maybe you should try forgetting this ever happened."

One of her eyebrows arched, and she pursed her lips. The expression made her appear amused, exasperated, and infuriated at the same time. Huh. In five minutes I'd managed to draw more emotion out of her than I had in the two years she'd run this school combined. Maybe she was dating. That always put my dad in a stellar mood.

"I don't think so," she said.

I shrugged. "It was worth a shot."

"Some kids are beyond redemption, but I don't feel that way about you. I think you can be salvaged." There was a long drawn-out pause as she studied my face, then said, "I'm going to take a day to think about the best course of action here. Tomorrow morning come straight to my office. Don't go to class, just come here. Understand?"

"Yeah." And I did. I understood perfectly. Waiting to hear the final verdict was part of my punishment. Which meant, not only did today totally blow, but tomorrow would, too.

Freaking great.

Just in case Ms. Hamilton called my dad, I avoided him for the rest of the day. I didn't go home, just called the house and left a message saying I was staying the night with Erica. Which was true. After school I piled in her rusty '82 Bronco and we eased out of the school parking lot, away from football practice and the cheering squad parading around in the field in their short shorts. Erica drove us to Café Giovanni—Italian for "young blood."

Situated dead center downtown, the café was underneath a towering redbrick building. A shadowed, winding staircase led to a small, dimly lit room that catered to the individuality I so loved. Pictures of vampires and witches decorated the walls, some for comic relief, others for the beauty of art. Soft, haunting music played in the background. Loreena McKennit, I think. Instead of traditional tables and chairs, black velvet and satin pillows were scattered across the polished wood floor.

We mostly came for the atmosphere. I mean, we were accepted here. No one ridiculed us or called us horrible names because *all* the patrons were Goths. Here, we were treated like equals. Here, we belonged. Here, we were able to relax and enjoy.

The owner, who was a flurry of movement behind the counter as he filled orders, thought he was a vampire. He'd had his teeth shaved into fangs and always wore a long, black cape. Everyone called him Count. I wanted to chuckle every time I said it. I mean, really. Hello, *Sesame Street.*

Erica and I claimed a corner space and spent several hours sipping crimson rivers (I swear there's not a single drop of blood in them, just fruit and spices) and chatting about the Gothic Martha Stewart website, about PC Cast (we both adored her books), and Lord Byron (thumbs-down from her, thumbs-up from me). Anyone who created such wildly romantic poems had my vote.

When we finished our last drink, we headed to Linnie's. Her "party" consisted of Erica, Robb, and me. Had she invited anyone else, they wouldn't have come. I was okay with that because I didn't need anyone else. Really.

We sat on the floor in her room, eating pizza and flipping through the newest copies of *Meltdown* and *Gothic Beauty.* Linnie's room rocked. Black crepe hung over the windows and chairs, casting eerie shadows over the faux-cemetery setting.

The walls were painted black—something my dad wouldn't let me do—with bare tree trunks etched throughout. Plastic stars glowed from the ceiling. Her bed's headboard was a simple wood carving with the word RIP dripping from the center in bright red. All around, dried roses spilled from vases.

Linnie is cemetery Goth.

Wait, that probably sounds weird. Let me explain. There are different types of Goth: Oriental, diva, dark fairy, cyber, Kindergoth, Egyptian. You name it. I'm punk Goth. Like Count, Robb is vampire—not that he actually drinks blood. He hasn't shaved his teeth, either, but he does wear plastic, attachable fangs most days. Thankfully, he's not wearing the fangs right now, which means he's not talking with a lisp.

Erica is cyber Goth, a lover of all things futuristic. She usually wears latex and rubber dresses, very I-belong-on-a-ship. Sometimes she even wears a silver full-body suit that makes her look like a space explorer out of a sci-fi movie.

"Ms. Hamilton both sucks and blows," Erica said, leaning against the edge of the black velvet settee, a piece Linnie's parents had purchased from a funeral home. She flicked her bottle-bright red-orange hair over one shoulder. "I can't believe she suspended Linnie for calling Mercedes a mad cow. That is so not fright."

"I called Mercedes a mad cow that needs to be exterminated," Linnie added happily. "Hammy said my words were tantamount to a death threat and I'm lucky I wasn't arrested."

She paused. Grinned. "This no-tolerance policy is absolutely delish! While you losers are studying and taking quizzes, I'll be clubbing all night and snoozing all day."

Erica gave a little pout. "Presidential elections are in two days. You won't be there to vote against Mercedes."

"Doesn't matter if Linnie is there or not," Robb said, his tone a bit dark. He eased onto his back, crossed his arms under his head, and stared up at the ceiling. "Mercedes will win. She always does."

Linnie's grin took on an evil glint, revealing the perfect white teeth her parents had paid a fortune for. "During lunch, one of you should put a laxative in her drink. She'll miss her own acceptance speech."

I laughed, picturing the queen Barbie stuck in the bathroom at school. Yeah, I was feeling a little more antagonistic toward Mercedes than usual. What exactly had she told Clarik about me? Whatever it was—I picked my nose? Peed the bed? Had ten thousand diseases?—he'd believe it. An *angel* like Mercedes would never lie.

Bitch!

"I should have run against her," Erica said, pensive. She plucked at the ends of her hair. "I want to vomit every time I see her."

"As if anyone would vote for you. Or any of us, for that matter. We're the most hated kids in school." A trace of bitterness layered Robb's words. "We might as well join the Chess Club."

"We're already freaks," Linnie said. "Do we really want to be losers, too?"

Robb's lips parted on a sigh. He wasn't a bad-looking guy. He had dark hair, dark eyes, and a strong face, but he was pale, tall and skinny, and completely uncoordinated. The Barbies liked to call him Stilts. He never said it aloud, but I knew the name embarrassed him.

"No way I'd want to be class president," I said. "Can you imagine having everyone in school come to you with their stupid problems? 'Ms. Hamilton gave me a tardy, waaah.' 'Mr. Parton yelled at me, boohoo.' 'I want chocolate cake served at lunch so I can throw it up in the bathroom later, sniffle, sniffle.'"

Robb snorted.

Erica bit into another slice of pizza.

Linnie's grin widened. "Drama, drama, drama. I swear to God I'd love every second of it."

I rolled my eyes. "Liar. I know you. You'd drug yourself to numb the pain, and when that didn't work you'd kill yourself because you'd claim hell would be way more enjoyable."

"Please. I'd have minions to do my evil bidding." She rubbed her hands together in glee and pretended to command her minions. "You, superglue Mercedes's hands to her desk. You, slash Avery Richards's tires. You, get Bobby Richards's drunk, cover him in chocolate syrup and ants!" She shrugged. "What's not to like about that?"

"Whoa." Erica grinned. "Not repressing too much anger, are we?"

"You are pure wicked," Robb said, tossing a beaded pillow at her and smiling for the first time that day. Linnie easily ducked. "But that's why I like you."

I'd been in the process of reaching for another slice of pepperoni but paused. I blinked over at Linnie, then Robb, then Linnie again. They were totally staring at each other. Linnie's cheeks were bright pink, and Robb's breathing was a little shallow.

I shook my head in shock. I'd never seen them look at each other that way. "Are you guys messing around behind our backs or something?"

Instantly Linnie's eyes narrowed on me, and Robb's expression darkened. "As if," Linnie grumbled. "He's like my freaking brother."

"Yeah," Robb said, glaring at the ceiling again. His lanky body was tense. "Her brother."

O-kay.

Maybe I should have kept my mouth shut, but I'd never been one to censor my thoughts or words. Besides, I'm not sure I liked the idea of Linnie and Robb dating. When they broke up—and they would; Linnie never dated anyone more than a few weeks (where she found her boyfriends, I didn't know)—Robb would hate her. She would hate Robb. And they would both insist Erica and I take sides.

Our group would never be the same again.

That wouldn't be a problem, except I *needed* the group. They were the only real friends I had. They were like my family. When my mom died, they comforted me. My dad had been a mess and had barely been able to take care of himself, let alone his teen daughter. I'd never forgotten and would never forget how these three had supported me.

"I watched the Barbie clones meow it today over that new kid," Erica said, thankfully changing the subject. "What's his name? Cary? Marick? Clarik. That's it! Clarik. They were pulling hair, scratching." She chuckled. "They even rolled on the ground like mangy animals. It was totally *National Geographic,* uncensored. I only wished it lasted longer."

My ears perked, and I leaned toward her. "What happened to Mercedes?"

"Nothing. Unfortunately." Erica pinched a mushroom from her pizza and popped it into her mouth. "She kicked major ass, and as much as I hate to admit this, she impressed me. The day you tore her up, she just laid there and took it. Not today, though. She fought like a jungle cat starved for fresh meat."

"Speaking of the day you tore her up . . . that was, like, the best day of my life," Linnie said with a chuckle. "Jade walked away with busted knuckles, and Mercedes crawled away with a broken nose and swollen eyes."

"What did Clarik do during the fight?" I couldn't help but ask. If anyone noticed my eagerness, they didn't comment.

Erica's shoulders lifted in a shrug. "He ate it up. Grinned the entire time and made no effort to stop them."

For the first time that day, I experienced a ray of hope.

Maybe Clarik didn't like Mercedes. Maybe he recognized her as rotten fish wrapped in a Krispy Kreme coating.

Maybe there was a chance he could like *me*.

Before I could explore that thought, Robb nudged me with his knee. When my gaze met his, he said, "I heard you were sent to Hammy's office today. What punishment did you get this time?"

"She needs time to think about it," I said darkly. "I find out in the morning."

"I bet she spanks you," said Robb. With a leer. Boys will be boys, I guess.

"I bet she calls your dad in for a conference and *he* spanks you," said Erica.

"I bet your dad sends you to military school," said Linnie.

"Look, Hammy isn't going to do anything and neither is my dad." It was a lie—and we all knew it. My stomach rolled into little knots. My dad wouldn't yell when he found out about my confrontation with Mr. Parton or anything like that. Oh, no. He'd just look at me with utter disappointment. He'd shake his head and say he had raised me better than that and my mom would have been ashamed. Twisting a knife in my heart would be less painful. "Let's talk about something else."

"Like what?" Erica asked.

"Like the color of Robb's underwear, for all I care." I shrugged. "Just something else."

Robb's brows arched and there was a wicked twinkle in his eyes. "Uh, who says I'm wearing underwear?"

"Ew, gross." Chuckling, Linnie threw the pillow back at him.

Erica threw a pillow at me, and it hit my shoulder. The fight was on then. Amid gales and squeals of laughter, pillows shot from one corner of the room to another, black blurs of silk. For a little while, I almost forgot about my upcoming meeting with Ms. Hamilton, my soon-to-be-dished punishment, and my dad.

Almost.

When we ran out of energy, the four of us plopped onto the floor. We stayed like that for a long while, panting and trying to catch our breath.

"Let's use my cards to find out how much trouble Jade's going to be in," Linnie finally said.

I groaned. "I thought we'd closed that subject."

"Not yet." She hopped to her feet and strode to her desk. Tarot cards in hand, she eased down in front of me. "Shuffle them." After I shuffled the cards, she began laying them out in front of me.

Silence. Dark, heavy silence.

I didn't bother sitting up, didn't bother looking at the cards—too afraid of what I'd find. A tremor worked through me.

Linnie hissed in a breath.

"What?" My gaze jolted to her. She'd gone pale, and her lips were pressed into a thin line.

Before I could glance at the cards to at last see for myself, she gathered them up. "Nothing," she said. She uttered a nervous laugh. "Nothing. Just . . . maybe don't go to school tomorrow."

"What did you see?" Erica asked her.

Linnie bit her lip. "Bad things. For all of us."

chapter three

When you know something bad is going to happen, does trying to prevent it from happening really help? Or does the bad thing happen because you tried to prevent it?

Tomorrow came too freaking bright and early. I'd lain awake all night, Linnie's words echoing through my mind: Bad things, for all of us. What did that mean? All I knew was that her cards were never wrong. They'd predicted Robb's mom and dad would divorce. They'd predicted Erica would be sent away to stay with her grandmother last summer.

Neither Erica nor I spoke of the cards as we drove to school. We didn't talk about anything. Just as the first bell screeched to life and the halls quieted, she waved good-bye, her expression grim. I entered the school lobby with dread. I wore astronaut pants and a slick, silver shirt, neither of which were mine. Since I'd stayed the night with Erica, I'd had to borrow her clothes.

Ms. Hamilton's office door was closed. I stopped and glanced at Cher. "She's expecting me. Can I go in?"

"Nope. Sorry." Cher shook her head, red curls flying in every direction. A pitying half smile raised the corners of her lips. "She's talking with your dad."

My dad? My mouth fell open, and I think my heart stopped beating. Please tell me she did not just say *my* dad. "How long has he been in there?" I squeaked.

Cher shrugged. "About thirty minutes is my guess. The good news is I haven't heard any shouting."

Yeah, that's a real silver lining.

"And just so you know, Mercedes's mom is in there, too," Cher added. "So have a seat; Ms. Hamilton will let you know when she's ready for the two of you."

Mercedes's mom? The two of us? Confused, shocked, and filled with more dread, I pivoted on my heel. The first thing I noticed was that Mercedes occupied one of the seats. Despite the two scratches on her cheek (gold star for whichever Barbie gave them to her) she looked prettier than ever in a pink sundress with her hair clipped back. She kept her gaze away from me and on the side wall.

My feet remained locked in place. My hands fisted. "Why

are our parents in there together?" I hated speaking to her, but my curiosity was too great.

"Fuck off," she muttered, twirling the ends of her pale hair. Her knuckles were layered with bruises.

The door opened and suddenly I could hear a symphony of amused voices. One deep, one monotone, one almost like a wind chime. There was no time for me to relax, because the laughter cut off the moment my dad stepped out of the office. Instantly his gaze locked on mine, and his smile vanished. Fury seethed under the surface of his expression and in his green eyes.

"Jade," he said, his tone hard.

I gulped and tried to play it fright. "Hey, Dad."

A pretty, petite blonde stepped to the side of my dad, her hands fisted on the waist of her expensive blue pants suit. Mercedes's mom, Susan Turner. I'd seen her around the school a couple of times, and at games as she watched her daughter cheer; she was always bubbly and upbeat. Now she glared at Mercedes. "I'm ashamed of you, young lady."

"Then we're even," Mercedes snapped, shoving to her feet. "*Middle-aged woman.*"

Mrs. Turner flushed and pursed her lips. "You don't talk to me that way."

"Really?" A tinkling laugh floated from Mercedes, somehow mocking in its airiness. "That's funny, because I just did."

A heavy silence blanketed the room, as if no one knew how to respond to Mercedes's daring. I couldn't believe she'd talked to her mom like that. Didn't she know how lucky she was, to have a mom who cared about her?

My dad and Mrs. Turner shared a heavy look before he turned his attention to me.

"I'm tired of the way you misbehave, Jade, and I've had enough. Ms. Hamilton is taking you on a field trip," he said, adding harshly, "You're lucky I don't send you to boot camp. You do not talk back to your teachers."

"A field trip?" My mouth fell open. Of all the things I'd expected him to say, that wasn't it. Trickles of relief swept through me. "Where to?"

"Somewhere you'll learn to appreciate how good you've got it." He paused, a muscle ticking in his jaw. "I've already signed the consent form. You'll go without protest, is that clear?"

He radiated unbending authority, and I didn't even think to try and appear unaffected. "Yes."

"Yes what?"

"Yes, sir." As far as I was concerned, I was getting off easy. No grounding. No ten-page reports. No "your mom would have been upset." So protest? I don't think so. I might even sing a chorus of hallelujah.

"You're going, too," Ms. Turner told Mercedes, "and if I ever hear about you conducting yourself so, so—"

"Can we get this over with or what?" Mercedes interrupted in that same breezy tone. She flicked her hair over one shoulder. "This conversation is boring."

Mrs. Turner gasped, the sound layered with a combination of outrage and sadness. "Yesterday you were caught fighting. Then, as if that wasn't bad enough, you were later caught engaging in unladylike conduct with a boy. In the library, of all places. And you dare to give *me* attitude? Is this the kind of example you want to set for your little sister? She looks up to you."

The beginning of Susan's speech cut through me, because I knew exactly what her words meant. "Unladylike conduct with a boy" equaled Mercedes making out. Having heard nothing about it yesterday—and I would have, since the gossip train never stopped running—it had happened sometime after she'd escorted Clarik to his classroom. That meant . . . A lethal blend of ice and fire traveled through me.

That meant Clarik had had his tongue down Mercedes's vile throat.

My stomach churned with sickening disappointment, killing all sense of hope. He hadn't liked me at all, wasn't interested in me in any way.

He was cute but I barely knew him, I reminded myself. This didn't matter. They didn't matter. *He* didn't matter.

Yeah, keep telling yourself that and maybe you'll start to believe it.

"—want you to come home directly after school," my dad was saying.

I forced myself to listen, to concentrate on him, to forget about Clarik. "I'm sorry. What?"

He frowned. "You and I are overdue for a talk, so I want you home after school." With barely a breath, he said, "Susan, I'll walk you to your car." He gently wrapped his fingers around Mrs. Turner's upper arm. He appeared very comfortable with her, completely at ease, as if he'd known her for a while.

I couldn't remember them having met before. At the moment, however, I didn't care if they were best freaking friends. Mercedes and Clarik had kissed.

"Ms. Hamilton can take it from here," he finished.

Mrs. Turner nodded and turned away from Mercedes. With a final glare at me, my dad ushered her away. Ms. Hamilton stood in the doorway of her office for a long while, silently staring Mercedes and me down, one at a time.

"You're probably wondering why you're being punished together, when your crimes have nothing to do with each other," she said in that monotone voice of hers. "I've had ongoing trouble with both of you, for different reasons, but the same punishment is appropriate."

"Where exactly—" Mercedes began.

"No more talking," the principal said. "Let's go."

Keeping my gaze away from Mercedes, I squared my shoulders, straightened my chin, and followed. I didn't need a new perspective on life and didn't know how Hammy actually thought she'd give me one on this "field trip," but I wanted out of this building. I wanted to get away from Mercedes and the knowledge that she'd kissed Clarik before I did something stupid—like cry.

• • •

I anticipated driving through slums, maybe to a crackhouse or a home for teenage parents so I could see how "good" my life was.

I anticipated wrong.

In total silence, with not even the hum of the radio, Ms. Hamilton drove us to a crumbling brown brick building on the edge of town. Mercedes claimed the front seat, leaving me the back. I wish I'd brought a notebook so I could write, take my mind off Mercedes and Clarik, my dad and Hammy. *Everyone.*

Several cars—all expensive and pristine—lined the dirt and gravel parking lot. The SUVs and luxury sedans didn't belong in the poverty-stricken setting. A few other buildings were nearby, each more dilapidated than the next. Graffiti and trash abounded. Broken glass. The faint echo of shouting and car alarms.

What was this place? I could not guess how it would teach us any kind of lesson except to avoid the area for the rest of our lives.

"You'll thank me for this one day," Ms. Hamilton murmured, exiting the car. "Come on. Let's get this over with." She sounded resigned, hopeful, and eager all at once.

Mercedes and I emerged warily from our prospective sides and trudged behind her. Sunlight glared down and should have heated the air, but a surprisingly cool breeze danced around us.

Get out of here, whispered across my mind and made me shiver. I gulped and entered, anyway. I'd promised my dad I would behave, so I would. No more trouble for me, thank you very much. Besides, what could Ms. Hamilton really do to us? Nothing, that's what. She couldn't hurt us without risk of being sued.

The moment the entrance closed behind the three of us, four tall, mean-faced men dressed in blue scrubs unfolded from a couch and chairs—as if they'd been waiting just for us.

They didn't say a word.

I watched in shock as two of them grabbed my arms, their grips steely and unrelenting. My eyes widened; my heart kicked into overdrive. "What do you think you're doing? Let go!"

The other two men latched onto Mercedes. She screamed like a baby in full tantrum and started kicking. "Let me go! Stop! I said let me go!"

"Calm down," Ms. Hamilton said with admonishment. "You brought this on yourselves, girls."

In that moment, I realized what was going on. My eyelids narrowed to tiny slits, and I stilled. "Are you trying to scare us straight? Is that it? Well, you'll have to do better than this to scare me."

"Oh, I will." Ms. Hamilton slowly smiled, a gleam of relish in her eyes. "Take them to their rooms."

Mercedes was dragged to the left, and I was dragged to the right. She protested but I remained silent, hoping I projected an unaffected air. My "escorts" pushed open double doors and a hospital-like room came into view, complete with monitors, railed bed, and a silver-haired old man in a lab coat.

He motioned to the bed with a tilt of his chin. "Strap her down."

Strap her down. His words reverberated in my mind and panic suddenly exploded inside me. Strapping someone to a bed stepped over the "scared straight" line. Way over.

"No, no, no," I shouted, jerking into fight mode. But even bucking wildly as I was, I was lifted effortlessly and lowered onto the bed. Seconds later, my wrists and ankles were bound to the railing with stiff, thick cloth. My heart slammed against my ribs in an erratic, dizzying beat. "Let me go. You can't do this!"

"This is Dr. Laroque," Ms. Hamilton said. The silver-haired man nodded to me. "He's in charge of your case and he can strap you down if he wants." With that, she strolled from the room.

Ohmygod, ohmygod, ohmygod. "Ms. Hamilton. Ms. Hamilton! Come back here! You can't leave me like this!"

"This will only hurt a second, Jade," the doctor said.

"Hurt?" Ohmygod, ohmygod, ohmygod. I shook my head violently, straining against my bonds. "Call my dad. Call him right now. He would never, never, never agree to something like this."

"You'll barely feel the needle, I promise."

"Needle?" Ohmygod, ohmygod, ohmygod. "Ms. Hamilton! Ms. Hamilton!"

"Don't worry. She's watching behind the glass." He arched a thick silver brow and pulled the plastic casing from a long—very long—needle. "Just relax. This is for your own good."

"Stay away from me." Riding a crest of fear, I arched and bucked. Despite my struggles, I remained locked in place. Helpless, not knowing what else to do, I bared my teeth, raised my head, and glared at the doctor. "You come near me with that, and I swear to God, my dad will kill you. He's military. He knows how."

"Your father signed the consent form," was the patient reply.

"Ms. Hamilton tricked him. I know it."

"Probably, but that doesn't change the fact that he did, indeed, sign the form." The doctor's movements never faltered as he hooked one end of the needle to a thin white tube. He stepped toward me. In the background, I heard Mercedes sobbing.

Ohmygod, he was going to do it. He was actually going to stick me with a needle. "I promise I won't talk back to Mr. Parton again," I rushed out. "Just get my dad. He'll—ow!"

"He'll applaud the change in you when this is over," Dr. Laroque said, inserting the needle into my arm.

I tried to scramble away from him, to twist to my side, to dislodge the tip. No luck. "You can't do this. It's illegal. You'll go to jail."

"Be still. The more you move, the more it will hurt."

"Just get away from me. Please," I added in a frantic whisper. Nearly a whimper.

A pause. A flick of his wrist. "There. We're done with the IV." As he spoke, he removed a syringe from his lab coat pocket.

Another needle? My eyes widened, and I fought yet another wave of panic. "What are you doing? What's that? I refuse to allow— Hey, stop that. Put the cap back on that thing. I said—stop leaning toward my arm. Stop—"

He slid the needle into the hub of my IV and shot me full of God knows what. My arm burned as he tossed the used instrument of death into a nearby sharps box and grinned down at me with satisfaction. His weathered, wrinkled face should have appeared as innocent and sweet as my grandpa's, and *would* have, if I hadn't mentally painted him with horns and fangs.

"There. Don't you feel silly for acting so childish?" he asked.

The fire that had been injected into me quickly spread, heating me. Scorching me. Burning me from inside out. The flames licked every inch of me. Tears pricked the back of my eyes, but I fought them back, gritting out, "I feel like you covered me with gasoline and lit me on fire."

He chuckled. "That feeling will pass."

Before he uttered the last word, the burning subsided as quickly as it had begun. My limbs relaxed into the cold, flat table. My muscles liquefied. At least he hadn't lied about that. A thin fog began to drift through my mind, and I fought to stay coherent. "What did you inject in me? Battery acid?"

"Silly girl. A sedative."

"Like that's any better." A strange weakness had already replaced the burning, growing, growing. "You're going to prison for a long, llllong time."

"Perhaps I'll be commended. Perhaps I'll be rewarded. You see, I've developed a virtual reality program that will whisk teenagers inside a new life—a life that will make them appreciate and respect the one they currently lead."

My nails dug into my hands, cutting into the skin. *Stay strong. Stay awake.* I had to get out of here. He was crazy. Insane.

"You don't believe me now," he said, "but you soon will."

Fight. Escape. I tried to jerk my hands out of the bonds, but didn't have the energy. So . . . tired. I was becoming boneless and sinking into a wide, welcoming black hole. "I just want to go home. Please."

"You'll be fine," he said, completely unmoved by my plea.

Two nurses approached me, one taking my left side, the other my right. Each masked woman attached tiny black clamps on my ears, then attached the other end to a computer. Soon a slight vibration sidled along my jaw line, up my temples.

"What are those?" My eyelids closed of their own accord, but I forced them open, forced myself to speak. "Take them off." My voice was slurred. "Please take them off."

"We can't." He anchored a surgical mask over the lower

half of his face. Only his eyes remained visible, and the determined gleam in them gave me no comfort. "The process has already begun. I want you to relax now," he said. He injected something else into my IV.

The lights dimmed, creating a soft golden glow. Sweet, humming music suddenly trickled from invisible speakers, the sound seemingly all over the room yet nowhere. "Close your eyes and relax," he added. "Your blood pressure is high. I want to bring it down before we send you into the program."

"Wait. Send me where?" *Please say home.*

"You'll see."

He wasn't going to relent. Wasn't going to free me. A shiver of cold racked me, chasing away the lingering heat in my blood. I wanted my dad. I wanted my mom. God, I missed her so much. I wanted . . . sleep. My eyes closed; my head lolled to the side. No. No! I jolted my head straight and pried my eyelids apart. Must stay awake. "How—how long do I have to stay here?"

"As long as it takes," was his only answer.

As long as it takes . . . I should be alarmed, I knew I should. Why wasn't I alarmed anymore? I heard the *beep, beep* of monitors, and breathed in shallowly the frigid, sterile air. A white ceiling loomed above me, the streamlined purity of it marred by the occasional camera, all of which were pointed at me. "Have you done this to other kids?" Good. I needed to concentrate, to focus. Keep the conversation going. "Has anyone died from this?"

"You're not going to die, I promise you." He glanced at the monitor nearest me and nodded. "Excellent, your blood pressure is coming down." Without another word to me, he moved toward one of the computer consoles. His fingers flew over the keyboard.

A group of people continued to bustle around me, clamping various parts of my body with the vibrating thingies. Tired. So tired. Unable to fight it any longer, I closed my eyes. My eyelids were simply too heavy to hold open a moment longer.

Breath shuddered in and out of my lungs. In and out. I needed something to occupy my mind. Something, anything to block the faint pitter-patter of footsteps, the medical murmurings, the increasingly slow *beep* from my monitor. The— wait. Was that Mercedes I heard cursing from the other room?

"All right, Jade," the doctor said. "You're ready." He sounded far away, and his r's reverberated continuously through my mind.

I tried to open my eyes again, but my eyelids were still too heavy. So heavy, in fact, it felt as if giant rocks now held them down. I frowned. What was happening to— Dizziness assaulted me, momentarily wiping conscious thought from my mind, leaving only darkness.

"I've placed another sedative in your IV. You should feel sleepy right now. Do you?"

I couldn't nod, didn't have the strength. I opened my mouth to say yes, but no sound emerged. *Daddy, where are you? Help me.*

"I'll take your silence for an affirmative," the doctor said, amusement dripping from his voice. "Get ready for the wildest ride of your life, my dear."

They were the last words I heard before oblivion claimed me completely.

chapter four

i'm not a bad person. i haven't killed any-
one. i (rarely) lie. i don't kick little pup-
pies. So why do people look at me as if the
world would be a better place without me?

Sunlight streamed through my red bedroom curtains. I'd wanted black cobwebs over the windows, I remembered groggily. My dad wanted me to have pink ruffles, a little girl forever. We compromised with blood red drapes. The crimson-tinted light stretched toward me, too bright, unwelcome, enveloping my bed and chasing away the thick fog in my mind.

I stretched my arms over my head and arched my back. God, I ached. My bones, my muscles, and my head throbbed like I'd been the meat in a three-car pileup—and two army tanks had been the bread.

Get up, Jade, my mind suddenly shouted. A wave of urgency rolled through me. *Get up! Something's wrong.* Slowly—and unable to force myself to move any faster—I blinked open my eyes. The intense light caused them to sting and water, as if I'd been in a dark cave for thousands of years and had only now awakened.

What was wrong with me? Was I sick? Hung over? No, couldn't be. I didn't recall drinking last night.

Last night: the phrase echoed in my mind, and I blinked. What had I done last night?

A knock sounded at my door—or was that knocking coming from inside my brain? I groaned.

Then I heard another knock. "Jade," a deep voice said.

My dad. I groaned again. If I ignored him, he might go away and I could sleep a little longer. I could—

"Jade?" his voice cajoled determinedly.

No, he wouldn't go away. "What?" I grumbled.

"Jade, sweetie. Time to get ready for school."

School. I jolted up in bed, my blue and black hair tumbling over my shoulders and into my eyes in a tangled mass. A wave of dizziness struck me, and I rubbed my temples. *Something's wrong,* whispered through my mind again. Wasn't my dad supposed to be mad at me? Instead, he'd sounded cheerful. And happy. I mean, please. Sweetie? I shook my head in confusion.

The action must have dislodged a memory, because I suddenly saw the flash of a needle, the grinning face of a silver-haired old man. I heard Mercedes sobbing and felt a strange vibration sliding down my spine. Mercedes . . . field trip . . .

Field trip! That was it. Like the flick of a switch, the entire event flooded my brain. Ms. Hamilton driving me to a dilapidated building on the edge of town. Dr. Laroque hooking me into his computer system, into a game he'd said, with the intention of teaching me to appreciate my current life. An IV, sedatives.

All of the frustration and fury I'd felt in the laboratory skidded through me anew. My gaze jerked to my arms, but I saw only the dark cotton of my favorite Grim Reaper T-shirt. With a shaky but determined hand, I slowly raised the left sleeve. No bruises on my wrist. Higher . . . a little higher . . . afraid of what I'd find . . .

I released a breath I hadn't known I'd been holding, the frustration and fury draining away. Not a single bruise or needle mark marred my skin. Relief pounded through me, sweeter than Bobby Richards's butt in football pants. Except, if I hadn't been strapped down, what had happened? My brow furrowed.

A dream, maybe? That was a possibility. A drug-induced trip into Crazy Town? But I hadn't doped up. I never did. Well, not anymore. The few times I'd tried it, I'd gotten crazy sick. Aliens screwing with my mind? I snorted. Truly, what the hell had happened?

Another knock on my door, this one harder. "Up and at 'em, sweetie. Time is wasting."

Sweetie, indeed. "I'm up," I called.

"Twenty minutes till breakfast. Don't be late."

"I won't." Pushing out a breath, I fell back onto my pillow and gazed up at my ceiling. Since yesterday—or what I thought was yesterday—hadn't really happened, today must be my meeting with Ms. Hamilton. I guess that meant I hadn't stayed the night with Erica and hadn't gone back to school the next morning to find my dad there.

How confusing. Still. One thing was for sure. After last night's imagined terrors, nothing Hammy did or said now could upset me.

I showered, dressed in my favorite plaid skirt and inky vinyl bustier, and anchored the blue streaks in my hair in two half ponytails. Needs something more, I thought as I studied my reflection in the mirror. I looped three silver necklaces around my neck, tugged on several bracelets, swiped my lips with blood-red lipstick, and spritzed my pulse points with the funeral-rose perfume Linnie had given me for my last birthday. *Perfect.*

Satisfied, I strolled to the kitchen.

Dad presented me with breakfast—a delicious meal of toast, eggs, and bacon, and I faked a grin in thanks. I had to fake the smile because, when I say "delicious" meal, I mean it sucks the big one. I hate, hate, *hate* my dad's cooking. Gasoline tastes better—but even that couldn't disguise the nauseating flavor of his "culinary genius," as he calls it.

I ate every dripping glob, though. Without complaint. I didn't want to hurt my dad's feelings. Once he'd coped with my mom's death, he'd done his best to take over her role as chef, chauffeur, and PMS advisor. Over the last two years, he's only gotten one of those right and I'll let you guess which one that is.

"So. What's going on in your life?" he asked, opening the morning paper.

I shrugged. "Same stuff as always."

He swallowed a gulp of orange juice and set his glass aside. He heaped a spoonful of (runny) eggs in his mouth, chewed, swallowed, and without looking up from his paper, said, "Are you going to drive yourself to school today?"

"Ha. You know I don't drive."

He expelled a sigh. "It's not healthy to fear something so much. You've got to get over that, Jade."

"I will." *Not.* "One day." And it would be the same day he found that money tree he liked to mumble about every time I asked for his credit card. Cars terrified me, okay. I paused, thought it over. Correction. Getting behind the wheel of a car terrified me.

I'd tried a few times since the accident, but had panicked uncontrollably and hadn't been able to even start the engine. The bloody image of my mom dying would fill my head, I'd hear the screech of tires, the grind of metal. I'd hear her scream.

I think my dad realized the depressing direction of my thoughts, because he quickly changed the subject. "You look nice this morning."

My fork froze in midair for the split second it took me to realize he was teasing. "Yeah. Right." I finished off that last (disgusting) bite and scooted the plate aside. If anyone looked "nice" today, it was *him*. As an aircraft engineer, he usually wore jeans and T-shirts. Today he wore black slacks and a matching, button-up shirt. Wait. He usually had Wednesdays off. Today was Wednesday, so he should still be in pajamas. "Are you working today?" I asked.

He didn't speak for a moment, then he folded his paper and set it aside. "No," he replied, and didn't elaborate.

"Are you going out?"

"Back up a minute, sweetie. Let's talk about you. I said you looked nice, and I meant it."

I rolled my eyes. "Whatever."

"Black is your best color, no doubt about it." As he gazed over at me, his features held a hint of wistfulness, an edge of sadness. "I wish your mom was here to see the beautiful young woman you've become. She'd be so proud."

This final bit of praise shocked me to the bone, and I blinked over at him. O-kay. Did he have a fever? Food poisoning? Brain aneurysm? My dad loved me, but jeez. I looked beautiful? My mom would be so proud of me? Black was my freaking best color?

One, he hated black.

Two, he never talked about my mom.

And three, he never—*never!*—complimented my appearance. In fact, he was always hinting I needed to change. For God's sake, the man bought me a pale pink cardigan, white Keds, and lace socks for my seventeenth birthday, hoping I'd suddenly forget about my affinity for vinyl, heeled boots, and fishnets.

"I'm ready for the punch line," I said.

His brow furrowed in confusion. "I don't understand."

"Neither do I. Are you playing a joke on me?" Or was this weird act some sort of punishment? Had Ms. Hamilton called him and told him about my confrontation with Mr. Parton?

No, surely not. If he knew about Mr. Parton, he would demand an explanation instead of . . . complimenting me. So. I guess that meant I had no answer and no idea what had brought this on.

"A joke?" He scrubbed a hand over his slightly stubbled jaw. "Why would you think that?"

I arched an eyebrow, shook my head, and said, "Answering my question with a question of your own. Good tactic, but it won't fly. Why are you messing with me, Dad?"

"Sweetie, I would never joke about that kind of thing. I know how delicate a young girl's self-image can be." He frowned, regarding me for a long, silent moment. "You're acting weird, honey. What's going on?"

"Case in point: 'sweetie' and 'honey.' You never call me by those names."

"I call you my sweetie every day."

I drummed my fingers on the tabletop. He had said that seriously, without a twinkle in his eyes or a hint of a smile curling his mouth. "Since when?" I demanded.

"Since . . ." Expression incredulous, as if he couldn't quite believe we were having this conversation, he threw up his arms. "Since forever."

"Dad. Please."

He shook his head and dropped his fork with a clang. "Are you and Bobby fighting again? Is that what this is about?"

"No, we're not—wait. What? Did you say Bobby? What Bobby are you talking about?"

"There's more than one Bobby in your life?" He chuckled. "Bobby Richards, silly."

I blinked, more confusion sizzling hot and bright inside me. Bobby Richards, the hottie jock all the girls drooled over? Bobby Richards, Mercedes's on again/off again boyfriend? Bobby Richards, captain of the football team and the boy I'd secretly crushed on for years before realizing how stupid such a crush was? My cheeks heated with just the memory of my foolishness.

My dad didn't know about Bobby. I'd never told him. I'd never told anyone. Not even Linnie or Erica. This past year, I'd even stopped thinking about him, had stopped writing stories about him.

"How do you know about Bobby, Dad? How?" I gasped,

a thought sliding into a place. "Did you read one of my note-books?"

My dad's mouth fell open in an affront. "I would never invade your privacy that way. You know Bobby came to the house last weekend. You were here. You invited him." Dad crossed his arms over his chest, concern darkening his eyes. "You're starting to worry me. Are you okay?"

"Stop it. Just stop." I didn't understand what was going on. Maybe he'd read the notebook, maybe he hadn't. Either way, why was he pretending I had a boyfriend? My confusion intensified. I was completely weirded out, and yes, angry, as I uncurled from the table. "I'm not sure I can deal with you right now, and I'm seriously considering calling your supervisor and recommending drug testing. Don't expect me home after school. I'll be with my friends." Without another word, I grabbed my backpack from the floor and strode out of the house.

"Sweetie?" he called. "Honey, what's gotten into you? Why are you acting like this? Talk to me. Please."

I kept moving, brushing past the white Jetta he'd bought me for my sixteenth birthday. I didn't slow my pace, even when he rushed onto the porch, staring after me. My bag, heavy with my books, bounced against my back. The thick straps dug into my shoulders. We lived a mile from the school, so walking was no big deal. I'd done it before. Thank-fully the morning air was clean and cool.

Desperate for an explanation, I replayed the conversation

with my dad through my mind. No answer magically appeared. Was I still asleep, perhaps, involved in a seemingly real nightmare?

It was just . . . my dad had never acted that way before. Never.

A car honked, breaking into my thoughts. Someone whistled. A girl shouted, "Hey, Jade!"

Startled, I glanced at the road only to see a Mustang convertible with two black-haired teens spilling from the windows. The car sped away before I could get a good look at the kids. O-kay. I shook my head, my confusion increasing yet another notch. I had no idea who had shouted at me. Not one of my friends, that was for sure.

Before I reached the school, three other cars honked at me. Two other girls and one boy belted out friendly hellos. It was . . . odd. Surreal. For God's sake, what was wrong with everyone today?

Finally, someone I knew drove past me. Erica. When I saw her Bronco, I experienced a wave of relief. I motioned her over, hoping to catch a ride with her and exit Bizarro World, like, yesterday. She slowed down, eased to the curb, and rolled down her window.

"Thank God you came by," I said on a sigh. "You won't believe—"

She flipped me off.

I ground to a puzzled halt, standing open-mouthed beside her car. "Erica?" Her name gasped from me. I could dismiss the finger as a joke. I could not dismiss her appearance, and I swallowed the sudden bile in my throat. Did I see pink? "Why are you dressed like that?"

"Rot in hell, Goth clone," she growled. Her tires squealed, rubber burning, as she peeled away.

Goth clone? Shock ripped through me as I watched her car disappear around the corner. What. The hell. Had just. Happened? Hate had gleamed in her eyes and seeped from her tone. Goth clone, I thought again, shaking my head. She'd called me a Goth clone, and she'd been dressed like a, a—I gulped—a Barbie.

I rubbed a hand over my eyes. I pinched my arm. Hard. I didn't appear to be dreaming right now. A blue sky and an ever-brightening sun still hung overhead. Lush green grass and cracked cement still held me upright.

If not for the Bronco, I wouldn't have recognized her. Gone had been Erica's silver makeup, bright orange hair, and piercings. She'd worn a buttercup yellow and pink polka-dot top. Her hair, a glossy sandy brown, had been combed from her face and clipped with a glittery barrette in the shape of a flower.

Okay. I'd seen and heard too many unexplainable things in too short a time, and suddenly felt a little disoriented, as if I'd stepped into some creepy, alternate—

By placing you inside the virtual reality game, I'll teach you to appreciate the life you have. Dr. Laroque's words drifted through my mind, and icy foreboding chilled my blood.

My eyes widened, my mouth fell open. No, no, no! my mind screamed. Sweat beaded over my skin. The virtual reality game had been a nightmare, a hallucination. Something like that. I didn't have needle marks. I didn't have bruises from the restraints. I *felt* real, as flesh and blood as always.

The denials rushed through me, loud, thankfully overshadowing the doctor's horrible, horrible words. I refused to believe I was trapped in a computer system. It was impossible. It was ridiculous.

Wasn't it?

Honk, honk, hoooonk. "I love you, Jade Leigh," a boy shouted, leaning out the back window of a sedan. "Will you go to prom with me? Please!"

"This is not happening," I muttered under my breath.

"Please," he begged again.

"This is not happening," I repeated. "Nope. Not happening." I didn't spare the boy a glance. Heart tripping in my chest, I sprinted the rest of the way to school.

chapter five

There's a really stupid saying: When life
hands you a lemon, make lemonade. Well, I
have a better saying: When life hands you a
lemon, shove that lemon up its stupid butt.

I arrived ten minutes late.

The tardy bell had already rung, and I was the only student in the area. I pushed past the double doors, sailed through the metal detector (and set it off, as always), and had to backtrack to be scanned—or be chased through the building, tackled to the ground, and carted to the nearest police station. Playing hide-and-seek with the guard wasn't on my to-do list today.

Frustrated, filled with a sense of urgency, I tapped my foot as I waited for the big, burly, always giving-me-grief security "expert" to grab the scanner.

"Hurry," I told him, adding, "Please," as an afterthought.

He smiled and waved me on. "I know you're not carrying a weapon, Jade, not a sweet thing like you. Go on. Get to class."

Sweet thing like me? No, no, no, I thought wildly and had to remind myself to breathe. He *never* dismissed me without hassling me. "I'm not inside a game," I muttered. "I'm not inside a game. He's just messing with me. Trying to get me in trouble."

If he heard me, he gave no notice. "Go on." His smile widened. "Get out of here."

My gaze remained locked on him for another split (seemingly endless) second, searching for answers but finding none. *I'm not inside a game,* I thought. "Fine," I grumbled. I rushed down the empty hallways. He didn't chase me. Walls, posters, and banners whizzed past. I was unsure, so unsure of what I'd find.

Panting—note to self: exercise more—I entered the office lobby. "I'm here for my meeting with Ms. Hamilton," I told Cher between breaths.

"I'm sorry." Cher hooked a red curl behind her ear. She looked normal, at least. A blood-red, sequined dress draped her plump body. "She's out this morning, doll."

Doll? I almost moaned. "When will she return?"

"She didn't say."

"Well, where is she?"

"She didn't say."

I threw up my arms. My jaw clenched and unclenched in frustration. "I have a meeting with her," I said, praying it was true, that yesterday had never happened and today was the real meeting. "She told me to come straight to her office this morning. So, here I am."

Cher frowned. "Are you sure about that meeting? I don't have you on the schedule."

"Did you—did you see me in here yesterday, then?"

Her chin canted to the side as she studied me. "No. Why?"

Breathe, Jade. Breathe. If last night was indeed a dream, then it's good news she just gave you. "Will you tell Ms. Hamilton I need to speak with her when she comes in? It's urgent."

"Sure thing, doll."

"Just—" What? Hunt Ms. Hamilton down? Pinch me? Tell me why everyone is acting so strangely? Tell me that yesterday never happened? "Don't forget to tell her I need to speak with her. It's a matter of life and death."

Cher's lips twitched. "I'm sure it is," she said.

I tangled a hand through my hair. There was nothing more I could do here, nothing more I could say. But I wasn't ready to leave. I clung to a fragile hope that Ms. Hamilton would suddenly appear and tell me it was time for our meeting.

"You should probably go on to class," Cher hinted.

To buy time, I said, "I need a tardy slip." As I spoke, I stared at the glass doors, willing Hammy to appear.

Cher smiled indulgently. "Don't worry about it. I'm sure there's a good reason you're late, and your teacher will understand." She waved me on, just like the security guard had done and even repeated his words. "Get to class. You know Mrs. Collins doesn't like to start without you."

Since when did my history teacher need my presence to lecture?

"But—"

"Go on," she said, a little more stern.

Stomach knotted, I slowly ambled away. My gaze lingered on the front door as long as possible. I didn't know what I'd find inside the classroom where I was headed; I only knew I was scared. Had Ms. Hamilton told everyone to treat me like a pampered princess? Surely not. That seemed too elaborate, and I couldn't understand how that would teach me a lesson.

I needed to talk to Mercedes. She could confirm or deny the field trip.

A shudder slipped down my spine. The concept of seeking out my worst enemy for a conversation was foreign to me, and everything inside me gagged. But . . . what if we *had* been sent inside a virtual reality program? What if—

God, I didn't even want to think about it.

"Everything will be okay," I chanted under my breath. "Everything will be okay." I reached my first class all too soon and stood in front of the red-and-black postered door, my hand posed over the knob. What would I find inside? Please be normal, please be normal, please be normal.

With a shaky hand, I turned the knob, opened the door, and stepped forward.

Mrs. Collins stood at the head of the classroom and the moment she spied me, she stopped taking attendance. Utter silence. Wait, were those crickets in the background? Her dark brown hair was pulled in a tight ponytail, and she wore an ankle-length beige skirt and a white button-up shirt. Perfectly normal.

I sighed in relief.

"There you are, Jade." Her entire face lit in a happy grin. "I'm so glad you could make it. Come in and we'll get started."

Not normal. My relief twisted into uncertainty. "I don't have a tardy slip."

The entire class turned in their seats, facing me. I flicked them a quick glance, faced Mrs. Collins again, and then jerked my attention back to the kids. My eyes widened, becoming impossibly round. Shock pounded through me, more intense in that moment than all the other times combined. My mouth floundered open and closed as I stared in horror. Oh. My. Freaking. God.

No way I was seeing what I thought I was seeing. I blinked, then blinked again. Nope, no change. "What's going on?" I managed to gasp out. I switched my horrified gaze to Mrs. Collins, my shaky hand sweeping over the students.

Her smile slowly faded. "Nothing is going on. Why?"

Please, let this be a dream. My gaze skirted over every student present, and I realized it couldn't be a dream. The acid in my throat was all too real. The lead ball in my stomach was too real. Yes, this was real and so terrible I had trouble drawing in air.

They were dressed as Goths. Nearly all of them. Goth. Black clothes, bright, multicolored hair, piercings, and tattoos abounded. Some of the girls had painted teardrops on their faces. Some wore black lipstick. One boy, John Hodges I think, had wrapped thick silver chains around the entire length of his neck.

Almost every classmate, from the girl who liked to trip me in the cafeteria to the boy who once turned the note I'd written him into a paper airplane, were grinning at me as if I were a shiny new car. Paid in full. Keys in the ignition. Several of them were wearing the exact outfit I'd worn yesterday. A few of them were playing with tarot cards.

No way Ms. Hamilton could have convinced this many people to dress like me as a joke or a punishment. That meant . . . That meant . . .

"Hi, Jade," someone said, breaking the silence.

They all spoke up at once then, their voices blending together. "Hey, girl."

"Did you get my message? Want to go to the mall later?"

"Are we still on for tonight? My parents are working late . . ."

"Where did you get those pants? Soooo *fright*."

Fright? No way Hammy could have convinced this many people to be nice to me.

Clattering voices rang in my ears, and I covered my mouth with my still-shaky hand. Ms. Hamilton and Dr. Laroque had really done it. They'd—they'd—they'd sent me inside a virtual reality program.

Everything inside me screamed to deny it, but really, how could I? The proof was here, right in front of me. Smiling at me. Asking me out on a date. Telling me my clothes were fright. I hadn't wanted to believe it, but . . .

I truly was in the virtual reality game.

This kind of thing happened in my stories, not in real life. Not in *my* life. My heart skipped a beat, and my stomach churned with nausea. *A game.* A stupid game meant to teach me a lesson. I didn't—I couldn't—

"Jade?" Mrs. Collins said, padding toward me. Concern darkened her expression. "Are you okay?"

I backed up a step. "I'm fine," I lied, the words barely more than a whisper. I didn't know what to say, what to do. Stay? Run? Linnie was home, expelled. Wasn't she? I didn't know anymore, didn't know *anything*. Still. Maybe I could stay with her for a few days and figure out what to do about . . . this. Oh God. I clutched at my stomach.

"You're so pale. Would you like me to get you a soda?"

Like a soda would fix all my problems. I scanned the room in search of something, anything familiar. I saw several students eating candy bars and chips, their legs propped on the chairs in front of them. Eating wasn't allowed in the class-room.

I almost cried in relief when I spotted Robb. He sat in the back, his hair combed and not a strand out of place, his white dress shirt buttoned to his neck. Once again, my relief twisted into uncertainty. He was familiar, and yet *not.* He looked so *proper,* like he belonged in church instead of the classroom.

I stepped toward him, desperate for an anchor in the midst of such craziness. He turned away from me. "Robb," I said, the sound a little broken.

He remained as he was.

Another step. "Robb?"

"Leave me alone," he said, unemotional and uncaring.

Everyone in the classroom watched in abject fascination. I froze in place, unsure, confused, trying to understand. He wanted nothing to do with me, just as Erica hadn't when she'd flipped me off. So. The program—God, that sounded so weird—had turned the Barbies into Goths and the Goths into Barbies. Dear Lord. Did that mean the former Goths hated me?

Did that mean my *friends* hated me?

Yes. The truth struck me, stinging like the needle Dr. Laroque had used on me. In that moment I understood what the doctor had truly meant, how he and Hammy thought to punish me. This was my worst nightmare. Here, I had no friends. Here, *I* was a clone. I was just one of the crowd, float-ing in a sea of uniformity I'd fought for years.

Besides my friends—which I now didn't have—my individuality was the only thing I valued. The thing that gave me the most joy. And Dr. Laroque and Ms. Hamilton, dastardly duo that they were, had taken them away. All to teach me a lesson.

How dare they? How dare they!

Fury seethed and boiled inside me, overshadowing my shock. My fists clenched; my muscles bunched, readying for a fight. Those *assholes* were responsible for this. Every horrible second of it.

Mrs. Collins wrapped her fingers around my forearm and gently led me deeper inside the room. I offered no protest. Not to her. She'd done nothing wrong and was concerned for me in a way I desperately needed. Plus, it was in my best interest to stay at school. Ms. Hamilton would return—soon, I hoped—and she and I could chat. And by "chat" I meant dunk her head in the dirtiest, nastiest toilet until she sent me home.

"Come on, dear." There was an empty seat at the front of the class, right beside Mrs. Collins's desk. That's where she ushered me. "Have a seat," she said, "and I'll call for the nurse. You're getting paler by the second."

"No. No nurse." I shook my head and tendrils of hair slapped my cheeks. Not hard enough, though. I didn't wake up from this nightmare. These people . . . were they real or merely animations? They looked real. They felt real. Mrs. Collins's skin was warm against mine. The scent of her familiar, floral perfume smelled real as it filled my nose.

God, I just didn't know.

Whether they were real or not, I couldn't mention what had happened. Not to a nurse. Not to anyone. No, no, no. I could guess every possible reaction to the conversation.

Me: The world around us isn't real. We're inside a game. I swear.

Reaction #1: Hahahahahaha. Good one.

Reaction #2: Someone call for an ambulance. We've got a drug overdose in progress.

Reaction #3: Put your overactive imagination away, young lady. What do you think I am, stupid?

Mrs. Collins hesitated. "Are you sure?"

"Very," I said softly, breath burning in my throat. Having nowhere else to go at the moment, I eased into the chair and dropped my bag at my ankles. I felt sick.

"All righty, then," Mrs. Collins said. "If you're sure you're okay . . ."

I nodded, the action almost imperceptible. And a complete lie. I might never be okay again.

"I'll begin my lecture. Class, you're in for a real treat today!" Practically skipping, she returned to the head of the class. She frowned. "Stevie, put your lighter away. You too, Hannah. This isn't a concert. Now then. The Salem witch trials were indeed a battle between good and evil, just not the way you think. They were—"

I tuned her out and twisted in my seat, casting Robb a hard, insistent glance. *Look at me,* I silently beseeched. *Like me.*

The Asian Goth next to him—I didn't know her name,

only that she was a fake—threw a wadded paper ball that crashed into Robb's cheek. He flinched. Several people snickered, but Robb ignored them. I knew he wasn't unaffected, though. Red color stained his cheeks.

"Freak," the girl muttered. She crumpled up another paper and drew back her elbow, ready to launch.

"Stop!" I shouted. "Leave him alone."

She froze. Her horror-filled gaze locked on me, and she dropped her hand onto her desk with a thump. "I'm sorry, Jade."

The words were so foreign to me, it was almost like she was speaking a different language. When had a student ever apologized to me?

"Is something wrong?" Mrs. Collins asked. Her hands were anchored on her hips as she glared at Robb, as if he were at fault for the disruption.

"No," I said, not taking my eyes from him. A pause, heavy and tension-filled. Mrs. Collins shrugged, and jumped back into her lecture.

Robb never even glanced in my direction.

Look at me. I need you, I thought.

Nothing.

"Hey, why are you acting so unfright?" Avery Richards, Bobby's twin sister, whispered. "I called your Sidekick this morning, but you didn't answer. I e-mailed it, but you didn't reply."

Assuming she was talking to the Asian Goth, I allowed my

head to fall into my upraised hands. Defeat swamped me. I wanted out of this game! I wanted my friends back to normal, wanted my dad back to normal. I wanted my individuality!

"*Pst.* Jade. Are you even listening to me?" Avery tossed a pencil and it bumped into my shoulder. "Jade! For real, pay some attention to me."

Frowning, I raised my head. My gaze met hers because she was staring at me expectantly. "Are you talking to me?" I asked.

"Your name is Jade, isn't it?" Her perfect brows scrunched—and didn't she just look sickeningly adorable as a dark fairy Goth? Avery was Mercedes's closet friend and second in command of the Barbies. She usually wore an aura of smugness, a sundress, and perfectly applied makeup. Today she gazed at me with genuine sweetness, was draped in black cobweb lace, and had red and black glitter circled around her eyes like a mask.

"What's wrong with you?" she asked. "Why did you defend that freak?"

"He's not a freak," I snapped.

"Then what is he?" She didn't wait for my response. "Yesterday you hated him, and today you defend him? Did I miss something? Why don't you ask him to prom and ruin your social status forever?" she suggested dryly.

I turned away from her. Did I mention that I hate her as much as I hate Mercedes? While Mercedes has always taunted me, Avery has always ignored me as if I'm beneath her.

"Jade," she whispered. "I'm sorry, okay. I shouldn't have

said that. Like you could ever ruin your social standing." She paused, tilted her head. "Mrs. Collins is right for once. You *do* look ungodly pale. And not in a good, undead-vampire way, either. You're like a corpse."

"I feel like one," I muttered.

"Girls," Mrs. Collins said with an apologetic smile. "I don't mind if you talk but bring it down a notch, okay? This is the second time I've been interrupted." She flicked Robb a narrowed glance.

"Sure thing, Mrs. C.," Avery said. "By the way, you're on fire today. I mean, your lecture is sooooo fright."

"Thank you." She twittered with a happy grin and jumped back into the lesson. I'd always suspected she'd been a nerd during her high school years. That would explain why she was beyond happy when the popular kids praised her.

Avery leaned closer to me, saying in a fierce but quiet voice, "You're only like my best friend. Tell me what's going on with you."

I inwardly groaned. Her best friend? As if. Usually, in her mind, I was like mud caked on her three-hundred-dollar boots. Her change in attitude made sense, though. My real friends hated me. So why wouldn't my enemies adore me?

The realization only increased my determination to get home.

"You don't really mean that," I said, refusing to play along. "We're not friends." No game was going to decide who *I* liked. Nor was any game going to make me forget all the things Avery had done to me over the years.

Her brows furrowed together, and hurt gleamed in her eyes. "Uh, yes, I do. And yes, we are."

"Avery, trust me on this." I spoke the words without anger, explaining like a teacher to a student. "We've never been and we never will be friends."

"Why would you say something like that?" Her pretty features crumbled, the hurt in her eyes intensifying. She straightened in her chair. "Did I do something wrong? I apologized for telling you to date the freak."

"He's not a freak," I growled, ignoring her questions. There was no way to answer her. The past I remembered obviously wasn't the past she remembered.

God, I had to find a way out of this hell.

Someone tapped me on the shoulder. Dreading what I'd find, I slowly turned . . . and came face-to-face with Bobby Richards. My dread morphed into another round of shock. He'd dyed his pale hair and it was now so black it appeared purple. Black eyeliner edged the corners of his eyes. He'd even rimmed his lips with black. And he looked good.

"Mmm, you look good," he said, mimicking my thoughts. His heavy-lidded gaze pursued me. He radiated the supreme confidence of a guy who knew all the girls adored him. "We still on for this weekend?"

If I hadn't been convinced of the game before, I was now. Bobby Richards was talking to me. He hadn't called me a freak. No, he'd asked me out. Unbelievable. Butterflies fluttered in my stomach.

"Well?" he prompted hopefully. "Are we?"

I managed to gasp out, "This weekend?"

"Yeah. I'm having a little party."

"After the football game?"

"Good one. You know football is for freaks." He reached out and tucked a strand of hair behind my ear. "My parents will be out of town. Tell me you'll come or I might as well cancel."

Tell him no. You refuse to play along, remember? "I don't know," I found myself saying instead.

"If you come, I'll make sure you have fun." His voice dipped low with suggestion and promise. "We'll have a Ouija board and tarot cards and we can kiss all night long."

The butterflies' dance became frantic.

"Mr. Richards," Mrs. Collins admonished. "Voice down, please."

"If Jade agrees to come to my party on Saturday," he responded, "I'll shut up. I won't say another word the rest of class. But she has to agree."

All eyes focused on me. Even the teacher's, who had an isn't-this-so-romantic glaze on her face. I gulped and shifted uncomfortably in my seat. Bobby cared about my presence.

"Jade, what did I do to upset you?" Avery beseeched, cutting through the sudden silence. "I can't stand not knowing."

"Nothing," I said, because I'd rather focus on her than Bobby. "We're fright, okay, so drop it."

"Really?" Slowly her lips lifted into a relieved grin.

"Well, Jade?" Bobby prompted.

The classroom door burst open and crashed against the wall, saving me from a reply. I jumped. Several people gasped. Mercedes rushed inside the room, her eyes frantic, her expression wild. Her outfit was perfect, as usual—a white sundress and sandals—but her hair was tangled around her shoulders, as if she'd raked her hands through one too many times.

"Is Jade Leigh in here?"

"Freak alert," Bobby muttered.

"Anyone bring a tranq gun?" Avery quipped, back to her usual self, only she had a new target. "We need to put the Barbie queen out of her misery."

Gales of laughter erupted.

"Avery? Why didn't you pick me up this morning?" Mercedes stalked up to her. "I waited for you."

"Ew." Avery shuddered and turned away from her. "It's talking to me. Somebody make it stop."

Mercedes ground to a halt, her horrified gaze trekking over Avery. "Why are you dressed like a Goth?" Her voice was tortured. "I called, e-mailed, and texted you this morning, but you didn't respond."

"That's enough! Who do you think you are, disrupting my class?" Scowling, Mrs. Collins pounded over to her. "Go to the office, young lady. Right now. I will not tolerate this kind of behavior."

I leapt to my feet. Robb stood, too, I noticed, from the corner of my eye.

Mercedes spotted me. Our gazes locked, and she closed the distance between us. "You were there," she said, ignoring Mrs. Collins. "You know this is wrong. You're the only one who knows."

I nodded, swallowing the lump in my throat.

"You have to help me. Something happened yesterday. Something horrible and awful and terrible."

"God, what a loser." Avery threw an eraser at her. When it bounced off her nose, Avery laughed. "Get out of here. You're stinking up the room."

"You have to help me," she repeated to me, desperate. "I don't know what to do."

"You don't need *her*," Robb said, marching forward. He brushed past me and clasped Mercedes hand. "Come on. I'll take you home. I've had enough of the Goth clones, too."

I watched as Robb dragged Mercedes out of the classroom, too shocked to speak. Robb hated the Barbies as much as I did, but right now he looked like an avenging angel, protective and determined, willing to endure punishment to save his . . . friend? Of course. If my friends hated me, they now loved Mercedes. My hands clenched.

He'd once considered *me* the one in need of protection—not that he'd ever made a scene for me. How many shocks could one person take before their heart exploded from strain?

"—and you can both go straight to Ms. Hamilton's office," Mrs. Collins was saying. "How dare you burst into my classroom and disrupt my lesson. That kind of behavior is un-acceptable."

A part of me enjoyed seeing my worst enemy reamed. The other part of me *really* enjoyed seeing my worst enemy reamed. Too bad I needed to speak with that enemy. Like she said, we were the only two people who understood the wrongness of the situation. Maybe—God—maybe we could help each other.

I found my voice and shouted on a wave of desperation, "Mrs. Collins, relax! Mercedes, wait!"

Mrs. Collins gasped, but stopped her tirade. Chairs squeaked against the floor as everyone turned and stared at me, wide-eyed and slack-jawed. Even Robb. He paused, blinking over at me, unsure how to react to what he probably considered odd behavior for the fake me.

Fake me—yeah, that fit.

Mercedes ripped free of Robb's grip and faced me. "Do you know what's going on, Jade? Did they tell you what they did to us?"

"Mrs. Collins, I'll make sure Mercedes goes to the office," I said. I didn't wait for her response, just rushed forward, clasped onto Mercedes's forearm, and jerked her from the room. She followed willingly. Robb followed, too, slamming the door in Mrs. Collins's stunned face.

chapter six

*What makes big boobs and perkiness so
attractive to boys? I mean, really. Two
round, mounds of fat and a fake smile.
Yeah, winning attributes.*

I spun around, facing my friend—whether he liked me or not, he was still my friend—and said, "This is private, Robb."

He scowled and crossed his arms over his buttoned-up cardigan. "You don't want a witness to your crimes, more like. Well, guess what? You get one. Sades is coming with me and—"

"Who *are* you?" Frantic, exasperated, Mercedes threw her hands in the air. "Have we ever even met?"

Color faded from Robb's cheeks, taking his strength and

determination with it and leaving a whole lot of hurt. Then he squared his shoulders, his features tightening. "Why are you acting like this? You're my girlfriend. We—"

"Gross." Features disgusted, Mercedes backed away from him and held out her hands, palms out. "We are so *not* dating."

His pale face became pallid, and I could see the blue veins under his skin. "Robb," I said, moving toward him. Reaching for him.

"Shut up!" He didn't spare me a glance as he brushed aside my arm. "Sades?"

Mercedes pinched the bridge of her nose. "Will you just leave? Please!"

"Sades—"

"Don't call me that. I fucking hate that name."

Robb backed three steps away, staring at the girl with whom he mistakenly thought he shared some sort of past. Looking at his crestfallen expression, feeling the hurt he radiated, it was hard to convince myself he was merely an animation of the boy I knew and loved. Maybe these people *were* totally and completely real. Maybe they'd simply been given new memories.

Simply? Yeah, right. Nothing was simple here.

"Robb," I said, once again reaching for him.

Without another word, he whirled around and raced down the hall.

"Robb," I called and started to run after him.

Mercedes latched onto my arm with a viselike grip. "This is a nightmare, Jade. Everyone is Goth." She spat the last word as if it was poison. "Have you seen them?"

"I'm not blind," I snapped, whirling on her. I shook off her hold. She wasn't the only one suffering. "You should have been nicer to Robb."

"They hate me," she said, ignoring my words. "Me! Someone actually threw gum in my hair. And this morning my mom asked why I refused to dye my hair black. She even laid out a hideous black dress for me to wear." Her face wrinkled in revulsion, and she began pacing. "I refused, so she grounded me. She actually took away my car."

My eyes narrowed to tiny slits. "You didn't need to treat Robb like that. He was trying to help you."

"Will you forget about him for a minute and listen to me?" Back and forth, back and forth she stomped. "This place is totally insane. Have you noticed that nothing is right? Nothing is normal?"

"No," I said dryly. "I haven't noticed. I didn't have my bowl of Smart Girl cereal this morning."

"You don't have to be sarcastic." She flicked me an irritated glance. "For all I knew, you were as brainwashed as everyone else."

Okay. She had a point.

"What the hell is going on?" she asked, tangling a hand in her hair.

"Remember Dr. Laroque and Ms. Hamilton? Remember

our little field trip? They said they were sending us into a virtual reality game."

"I know, stupid! I was there. But this doesn't feel like a game. This feels real."

"I know," I said softly, fear tingeing the undercurrent of my voice.

"How do we get out of it? I can*not* stay in"—she spread her arms wide, encompassing the entire school—"Goth Land. Not that *you* want to leave," she added angrily.

"My best friends hate me, and I'm a freaking clone. I can't get out of this hell fast enough."

"Oh, sure. I believe that. Have you seen this?" She ripped a poster from the wall and shoved it at me. "This has got to be a little slice of heaven for you."

I glanced at it and my knees almost buckled. VOTE FOR JADE, it read. CLASS PRESIDENT. My own face smiled up at me. Same green eyes. Same slightly round cheeks. Same too-full lips. "You've got to be kidding me. Tell me you're kidding. Tell me you printed this yourself."

"Do you think I'd joke about class elections? That's supposed to be my job." Glaring at me, she pointed to her own chest. "Mine."

"You can have it," I said darkly, wadding up the paper. "I don't want anything to do with it."

"Please. Like I really believe th . . . that . . ." Her voice trailed off.

A boy—Clarik, I realized a moment later—had turned

the corner and was strolling in our direction, hands pushed into his pockets. I watched him, unable to look away. He was dressed in baggy black jeans and a white T-shirt that pulled tight against his biceps.

He hadn't colored his hair, I noticed. The brown waves tumbled over his forehead and ears. He was half-Goth, half-preppy, and it looked good on him.

My pulse tripped into overtime. It felt like it had been weeks since I'd last seen him, but it had only been a day. Then I remembered, *You don't like him, remember?* He kissed Mercedes.

He spotted me and slowly smiled that mysterious smile of his. "Hey, Jade." His eyelids lowered as his gaze swept over me. "Looking good."

"Hey, Clarik," I said, then cringed. I'd sounded like a breathless Barbie in full flirt mode. "You ditching?"

"Nah. I was lost," he said with a small amount of self-derision, "but I'm on the right track now."

"Hi, Clarik," Mercedes said with a finger wave. She gave him a forced grin.

He pretended she didn't exist, instead saying to me, "You going to Bobby Richards's party this weekend?"

You don't like him. "I don't know. Are you?"

"I might." He maintained his smile, but the closer he came, the more I noticed the hard glint in his blue eyes. Determined. Purposeful. What did that mean? "Maybe I'll see you there."

"Maybe," I replied. My head followed his every move as if we were connected by an invisible cord. Maybe it was bad of me to think this—boys got in trouble for this line of thought all the time—but he looked as good from behind as he did from the front.

"Clarik," Mercedes called, a desperate twinge in the word.

He kept right on walking.

"Clarik!"

Still nothing. He disappeared down the next hallway.

She screeched in frustration and whipped to face me. "Do you see? Do you see what I've had to put up with all morning? I'm the most popular girl in this shithole, damn it. People beg for my attention."

"You *were* the most popular girl in this shithole," I muttered, feeling the first stirring of satisfaction since I'd realized what had happened to us. For once, I wasn't the freak.

She gasped. She even took a menacing step toward me. "Why, you rotten little bitch."

I closed the rest of the distance until we were nose-to-nose. If she wanted to meow it, we'd meow it. "I merely stated a fact, *Sades*. Get over yourself."

"After the way you just ate him with your eyes, you can't expect me to believe you want to leave this place," she growled. "Admit it. You want to stay."

"I want to leave as soon as possible, and *that's* the truth."

Her eyes searched mine, gleaming with barely suppressed panic. I'd never seen her so distraught. I understood her panic, though. I felt the same way. Unsure, confused, mystified, angry. But I wasn't going to let her dump on me.

"How can I believe you? You're everything here, and I'm nothing," she said.

"I told you I want to leave, so you're just going to have to trust me. Instead of fighting, we need to figure a way out of this."

She paused only a moment before stepping away from me. She jerked another hand through her hair. "How? Ms. Hamilton is MIA and no one in the office will tell me where she is."

"Well, she has to return sometime. It's her job. The moment she gets here, we'll tell her to send us back."

Mercedes laughed, the sound devoid of humor and layered with bitterness. "And if she won't?"

"Let's . . . I don't know. I guess we go back to the lab and find that asshole doctor."

"I'm grounded, remember?" She slapped the row of locks hanging from the lockers. "My mom took away my car and expects me home right after school."

"Since when do you do what your mom tells you?" Sighing, I leaned against the wall, the wadded poster crackling between my fingers.

She eyed me warily. "What are you saying?"

"If Ms. Hamilton doesn't show up today, you're going to sneak out tonight and come get me. We'll find the lab, and then we'll find a way out of this. Until then, just smile and pretend everything's fright."

"Don't you mean 'cool'? Pretend everything is *cool*?" She shook her head. "Whatever. Sure, I'll smile."

"Yeah. Smile."

Sticking around the school and waiting for Ms. Hamilton— my smile never wavering—proved more difficult than anything else I'd ever done. But I did it. For the most part. I pretended like it was a nice, normal day, pretended like I wasn't wishing everyone who approached me would rot in hell, and smiled. And waited. And smiled some more.

And freaking waited some more.

By lunch, my smile was brittle and my pretend happiness on the verge of total annihilation. Allow me to explain why.

Number of times I was asked for outfit advice: 9

Friends who hated me: 2

Number of times said friends flipped me off: 10

Number of times kicked out of front office: 14

Homicides slimly avoided: 671

Smile, I reminded myself as I took my place in the lunch line. A boy skateboarded past me. I wanted to yell, "That isn't allowed."

Yesterday the entire school despised my hair, my clothes. Yesterday they called me bad names and laughed at me. *Yesterday* they would have killed themselves if they'd been caught talking to me. Today they loved me. Everyone knew my name, and everyone wanted a piece of me.

Everyone except the only two people who mattered, that is. Erica and Robb.

During my creative writing class—which had, surprisingly, been bursting with students—I once again approached Robb. He once again acted as if he didn't hear or see me. I'd wanted to shake him, but had been too close to tears. I was used to rejection, but not like this. Not by someone who was supposed to understand me.

The lunch line inched forward. *Smile, Jade.*

Lord, my face hurt. So badly I wanted to leave, to just pack it up and go somewhere, anywhere else. I couldn't, though. Where the hell was Ms. Hamilton? Hiding, most likely. Afraid we'd hurt her? Most definitely.

I didn't know how many more days like this I could handle. Please let her return today, I prayed, edging ever closer to the silverware. I wasn't hungry and didn't think I would be able to eat, but I was desperate for some sort of normalcy, something to ground me in my other reality. I always got a tray from this line; today would be no different. I hated this feeling of free-falling in a winding, dark, *unfamiliar* tunnel, twisting and turning.

The girl dressed as an Asian Goth passed me. "Darkness rules!" she cried, then stopped and backtracked. She had inky black hair slicked back in a bun and held together by chopsticks. She'd painted her face white and was wearing a shiny Kimono. "Are you eating a hamburger, Jade?"

I groaned inside. *Smile. This is a nice, normal day.* "Yeah. I am."

"Fright." Her mouth stretched in a wide grin, revealing silver braces. "Me, too." She clomped off to the end of the line, calling, "Did you hear that? I'm eating the same thing as Jade Leigh!"

Her excitement freaked me out. She wanted to be me, to take my identity—Miss Popular—as her own. They all did. "Why won't this line hurry?" I muttered.

The punk Goth in front of me spun on his heel. He reeked of tart cologne, and I wrinkled my nose. "You can go in front of me," he said. His eyes were wide and brown, and he looked like he'd just been given a naked cheerleaders calendar.

"That's okay." Smiling. I'm smiling. Nice, normal day. I shook my head. "I'm fine where I am."

"No, really. It's okay. It's better than okay. Please."

"I'm fine," I repeated. Why wouldn't they leave me alone? Just give me a minute or two of peace? At one time, I *had* wanted to know what it would be like to be popular, to be loved and included. How could I have known it would make me feel like I was being pulled in a million different directions? Like I was a fraud? Like I was someone other than myself? "Really. I'm fine."

"You can go in front of me, too," a girl said.

"Me, too."

"And me."

The line suddenly opened up. I gazed ahead, and for a surprising second (or two) I stopped feeling stressed and actually experienced a little delight. Because these kids liked me, I wouldn't have to stand in line and wait. I could grab my food and at last sit down and relax.

All too soon, however, I recalled how these same kids liked to push me and my friends out of the cafeteria, steal our trays, and trip us. My eyes narrowed on them.

"Jade Leigh shouldn't be at the back of the line," the punk Goth said.

This generosity would come with a price, I knew. These people—who only liked me because I was (supposedly) popular—would now expect me to treat them like a friend, to wave at them in the halls and talk to them between classes. No way. That would totally betray my true friends.

You hate me, and I hate you, I wanted to shout. But I moved to the front with my head high. No one attempted to kick or shove me. How that used to bother me. How I'd hated it. Now I almost wished they would do it; then I wouldn't feel conflicted in any way. I wouldn't want to smile and thank them for such a nice gesture. I'd just hate them like I normally did.

The scent of overcooked, greasy meat hit me. My stomach churned, but I collected my tray and turned toward the tables. My gaze skidded to my usual table in back. Robb and Erica were there, alone. They looked so preppy. I couldn't get over that fact. Thankfully, Mercedes was nowhere to be seen. I might have beat her up if she'd been with them, pretending to be their friend.

I straightened my back (smiled again) and stepped toward them. When I reached the table, I gently placed my tray beside Erica's. Startled, she glanced up. Her eyes narrowed, and she nudged Robb.

"Look who decided to slum it," she said.

Robb glanced at me, frowned, and jolted to his feet. "Why don't you go back to your friends, so you can curse us with your black magic or whatever it is you do. Just stay away from us."

"I want to sit with you, that's all."

"Leave us alone," Erica said.

"You like me," I found myself saying in a rush, hoping to make them understand, "but I was forced into a virtual reality game and it changed everything around." I had decided not to tell anyone, but I wanted so badly for them to know and like me again that the words poured out.

"My God." Erica glowered at me. "You actually think we're stupid enough to fall for that?" She flipped me off and stood.

Together, she and Robb walked out of the cafeteria without a single glance in my direction.

Hurt washed through me as I stared after them. I guess a part of me had expected them to remember (or realize) the truth by now. At the very least, to consider my words. My shoulders slumped, and I lost my smile. I couldn't force it to stay a moment longer, and I couldn't force it to come back. I haven't done anything wrong, I wanted to shout at them. How can you treat me like that? I wanted to scream.

How could they abandon me when I needed them most?

"Hey, Jade," someone said beside me. I didn't turn and look. "Are you participating in the fund-raiser for Wizardry

Club? We're selling coffin necklaces this year. They're really fright. I'll buy you one if you want."

"No, thanks," I said, distracted.

"Jade!" One of the Barbie clones—no, Goth now. The Goth clones—a.k.a. the Fake Goths—waved me to their table. "Over here, Jade," Avery called.

They were the kind of people others envied. They had everything: beauty, brains, and talent. Yet they tore others down, rather than build them up. And they expected me to be one of them.

Shaking my head, I lifted my tray and looked away. I couldn't be in their company a moment longer without killing someone. They'd dogged me all day, and had even followed me into the bathroom: "Do you like my hair? . . . Are my nails black enough? . . . Should I pierce my eyebrow? . . . Look at that freak."

Having trouble drawing in a breath, I continued my search. My gaze snagged on another group of people, the jocks. Well, they weren't jocks any longer. Word around the hall was sports were "out" and darkness was "in." I stiffened. They, too, waved me to their table. "Sit by me," Bobby said. He patted the empty seat beside him. "I saved you a spot."

Breathing became even more difficult. Again, I shook my head and looked away. I didn't know what I'd say to him. He made me nervous. The band geeks motioned me to join them. They still weren't popular, but they were higher on the social ladder than the Barbies.

All around me I heard, "Over here," and "Sit by me." The voices blended together and became a constant, blurred ring. Time slowed to a torturous dragging. I had no real friends. I was trapped here indefinitely. Waves of dizziness swept through me, and shallow puffs of oxygen burned in my lungs.

"We saved you a seat, Jade."

"Where did you get your shirt, Jade? It's so fright."

"Can I get you anything, Jade?"

As they called for me, my frustration, my fury, and my every suppressed scream flooded me, rushed me. Drowned me. Couldn't . . . breathe . . . at all now. This was too much. There'd been too many changes in too short a time. My world had been dumped upside down, cut up, and glued back together with the wrong pieces.

I needed to be alone. I needed to think. But every table was occupied, even the one I stood in front of, the one Erica and Robb had vacated only seconds before. I felt myself paling, felt sweat beading on my forehead.

Someone bumped into me, and I stumbled forward. Sliced pears swished over the rim of my tray.

"Watch ou—" I heard distantly. "Oh, hi Jade. I'm so sorry. I should have looked where I was going. Fright shoes. Where did you get them?"

I had to get out of here; I couldn't take it anymore. Couldn't take any more questions about my clothes or my favorite hair products. Couldn't take any more false smiles—my own or theirs—couldn't take any more false bits of praise.

I wasn't who these people thought I was. They didn't really like me, I mused again, they just thought they did. It was all so fake, no one and nothing true to itself.

"Jade?" someone asked, voice filled with false concern.

"Yo, Jade!"

I dumped my tray and ran. Just ran.

chapter seven

*How does fear become so powerful? We can't
see it. We can't touch it, yet it gets its
claws in us and begins to control us. Sigh.
I hate feeling afraid, and I hate, hate,
HATE feeling out of control.*

I made it to the parking lot before grinding to a halt. I didn't
have my backpack and didn't have any money. What's more, I
didn't have a mode of transportation.

I was stuck.

Hot, humid air beat all around me, sweltering, driving
home the point that I truly was in hell. Bending over and anchoring my palms on my knees, I sucked in breath after
breath of needed air.

I could have walked home, but I didn't want to deal with my dad's new appreciation for a girl that wasn't really me. Why couldn't he work a regular week like other parents, Monday through Friday?

I couldn't go to Linnie's. She probably hated me as much as Robb and Erica did.

"Hey, Jade."

No! I kept my head down, glaring at the gravel at my feet. The sun glinted off it, making me squint. If one more person asked what kind of hair product I used, I was going to give the students of Hell High another *National Geographic* demonstration. "Go away," I mumbled.

A pause. Then, "Fine. Whatever."

My eyes rounded, and I flicked a glance to the side. I recognized Clarik's jean-clad butt as he walked away from me. Recognized the deep voice that was echoing in my ears. Had he followed me out here? He had appeared as surely as if I'd cast a magic spell for him.

As much as I craved solitude, I found myself shouting, "Clarik!"

He paused. I straightened. Slowly he turned on his booted heel. One of his dark eyebrows arched under the fall of dark hair on his forehead. There was a flash of guilt in his expression, as if he were sorry for interrupting me. "Yeah?" he said.

"What—what are you doing out here?" I asked stupidly. I didn't know what else to say. My mind had gone completely blank.

"You looked upset. I thought I could, I don't know, help or something. Obviously, I was wrong." He turned to walk away again.

"Wait." Being alone didn't seem so wonderful all of a sudden. I'd just worry some more. Probably cry. Definitely contemplate the many ways to torture Ms. Hamilton. "Please wait."

Surprisingly, he did. He faced me, inch by agonizing inch.

"I'm sorry," I said, and I meant it. "You were being nice, and I was rude. It's just, well, this has been a really unfright—" Wait. I didn't want to sound like everyone else. "This has been a really crappy day." Understatement of the year.

He shifted on his feet and studied my face. I'd made him mad—or perhaps I'd hurt his feelings—when I told him to go away, but whatever he saw on my face (desperation, frustration, homicidal urges) softened him. "Do you want to get out of here?" he asked.

I blinked. "Out of here, as in, leave campus?"

"Yeah."

You need to wait for Ms. Hamilton . . . You need to talk to Robb and Erica . . . He kissed Mercedes yesterday . . . While my brain listed all the reasons I should stay, my mouth said, "I'd love to leave with you. Yes. Thank you."

"Come on." He turned, a silent command to follow or be left behind, and walked toward his car, an old rusty Dodge Dart.

I fell into step beside him. He was the first good thing to

happen to me all day, and I wasn't ready to give that up. So shoot me. (Please. Someone. Anyone.) I realized, surprisingly, I didn't feel stifled with him. Or fake. Or stressed. In this moment, I was just plain, ordinary Jade Leigh—a girl who wanted to spend time with a boy. As a friend. Only a friend.

"Where are we going?" I asked.

"To lunch." His lips curled into a half smile. "Someone once told me the food here sucks."

He remembered. I almost grinned. "How'd you get a pass?"

His smile grew wider. "I didn't."

"You, uh, know this is a closed campus, right?"

"So?" He opened the passenger door for me (how sweet!), and I slid inside. Foam protruded from a myriad of cracks, scratching my skin. I didn't care. Scratches were the least of my worries.

"How do you expect to leave without a pass?" I asked when he eased into his seat.

"You'll see."

Relaxing, I buckled up and settled into the lumpy cushion. Clarik smelled good, like soap and a hint of motor oil. I could feel the heat of his skin, could even hear the sound of his soft inhalations.

I'd never been this hyperaware of a boy before.

Part of the game, perhaps? If so, the doctor miscalculated the severity of my punishment because I actually liked it.

When Clarik keyed the ignition, heavy metal blasted from the speakers, startling me. I jumped and clutched at my heart. His grin turned sheepish, and he lowered the volume. "Sorry." He eased the car into gear. "Do you like Mexican?"

At this point, I would have agreed to eat chocolate-covered ants just to get away from the school. "Love it."

"Good."

A security guard stood at the end of the parking lot, waiting at the only exit. He wore his blue uniform proudly. His arms were crossed over his chest, his expression no-nonsense. I bit my bottom lip. Once I'd tried to leave campus without a pass—and spent an entire month in detention.

Clarik stopped at the barrier. As he rolled down his window, the scowling guard stalked to the side of the car. His dark mustache made him look all the more menacing.

"Where do you think you're going, boy?"

Clarik shrugged, seemingly unconcerned. "Out."

There was a tension-laden pause. Should I say something? Maybe I could talk the guard into letting us go. I mean, I was the darling of the school now. Why not use the power for something good?

"You plan on coming back?" was the growled response.

Wait. What? I blinked at the guard once, twice.

"I'll be back for next period," Clarik said, still casual. "Promise."

The guard sighed heavily, losing all hint of his upset. Now he merely appeared wary. "I could be fired for this, you know.

God Almighty, you're gonna be the death of me. It's only your second day here."

"The cafeteria food smelled bad."

Another pause, an eye roll. "Fine. Go on, then, but you better not be late for your next class. And you better be careful with the girl. I want her returned in the same condition you left with her or it's my butt they'll flay."

"No problem."

As soon as the barrier was lifted, Clarik sped onto the street.

"O-kay," I said, turning to stare at the guard through the rear window. "Do you have some sort of superpower I don't know about?"

"He's my uncle," Clarik explained with a laugh. "I live with him now."

"Oh." I shifted toward him. "Must be nice, having someone on the inside."

He snorted. "You make the school sound like a prison. But yeah. I guess it's nice."

The air conditioner seeped out, cool and welcome, and I felt myself sink into the uncomfortable seat. Leaning my head against the window, I gazed out the dusty glass and drank in the tall green trees, the black birds flying overhead. Oh, that I could fly away from this reality.

"So what's this I hear about you acting weird?" His voice cut through the silence, sliced into my reprieve. "You're all anyone is talking about."

"You wouldn't believe me if I told you," I muttered.

"Try me."

I'd decided not to tell anyone, and I wouldn't again. Not after the incident with Robb and Erica. Clarik would laugh. He might even accuse me of being wicked insane. I barely believed what had happened myself and I had lived—was living—through it. More than that, I didn't want to think about the game right now. This was my escape from the false reality and I wouldn't spoil it.

"So where are you from?" I asked, changing the subject. "And why'd you move here?"

He handled the change without comment. "I'm from Tulsa, but my mom—" His words jammed to an uneasy quiet, and his expression tightened. A moment passed. Then he shrugged, the action stiff. "Sh— We just decided it would be best if I moved up here and stayed with my uncle."

The way he corrected himself, changing "she" to "we" said a lot, and I felt a pang of sympathy for him. I bet he and his mom hadn't agreed it was the best thing for him. I bet *she'd* thought it was the best thing for him.

I couldn't imagine my dad not wanting me with him and actually kicking me out. I understood not wanting to talk about something, though, and didn't press him for more. "Do you work after school?"

His shoulders lifted in a shrug. "Weekends, I restore cars, motorcycles, that sort of thing. Weekdays, I work on computers. What about you?"

"Nope, no job. My dad wants me to enjoy being a kid before I enter the big bad world of employment. After I graduate, I'm sure I won't be able to get one fast enough to suit him. I want to write, so maybe I'll try to get one at a college paper or something." I shifted in my seat, trying to get a better view of him. "Do you play sports? First time I saw you, I had you pegged as a ball player."

"I did play football. I might play for Haloway, I might not. I haven't decided yet—and not because it's not a very popular sport or anything like that. I just, well . . ." He hesitated, coughed. "I was kind of kicked off my old team for playing too rough."

The fact that sports weren't popular still gave me a jolt. "I thought you were *supposed* to play rough. That's why everyone wears pads."

He flicked me an amused, you're-so-cute smile. "I never said the rough play was on the field."

I couldn't help but smile in return.

He looked from me to the road, from the road to me, then back to the road again. By the time he stilled, he was frowning, all hints of his amusement gone. "Are you and Bobby Richards, like, dating?"

I snorted in self-derision. "Hardly. He and Mercedes have—" Wait. Most likely here, in *this* messed-up reality, they haven't.

"I seriously doubt someone like Bobby would date someone like Mer . . . cedes," he finished lamely. He pressed his lips together, as if he realized he'd said something wrong and wanted to snatch back his words.

My entire body stiffened. Yesterday I'd been the "someone like Mercedes." I'd been the outcast, the girl everyone hated. Had Clarik thought that about me yesterday? That I wasn't good enough for Bobby? Wasn't good enough for him?

"Are you one of those popularity-obsessed guys?" I demanded. "If the girl doesn't hang with a certain crowd, you don't want to date her?"

"God, no," he said, disgusted.

"God, no, you're not popularity obsessed, or God, no, you wouldn't date an unpopular girl?"

"I'm not popularity obsessed. If I like a girl, I like a girl no matter who she hangs with." His frown deepened, branching lines of tension around his mouth. "What made you think something like that?"

"You said 'someone like Mercedes.'"

"Bobby seems nice. She . . . doesn't."

I relaxed. A little. "I don't know a lot about Bobby. Mercedes, well, she has her moments." Mostly moments of pure evil, but there for a minute, in the hallway, I'd glimpsed a more vulnerable side of her. A side I had, surprisingly, connected with.

"So you and Bobby aren't . . ." He trailed off.

I shook my head. "No." I admit, I had wanted to date Bobby at one time. I'd wanted it more than anything else in the world, in fact. Right now, I couldn't even picture Bobby's face in my mind.

It *soooo* wasn't smart to crush on Clarik like this. Okay. There. I'd stopped pretending I didn't like him as more than a friend. I was crushing. Hard.

"He talks like you're a couple," Clarik persisted.

"Well, he's wrong. And when did you talk to him? What did he say?"

"I talked to him this morning, during third period, and he said you guys were . . . you know. More than friends. Friends with major benefits."

I gasped, horrified. "I have never slept with him!" I paused, a thought hitting me. "Is that why you're taking me out for lunch? Because you think I'm easy?"

Clarik scowled. "You begged me to bring you, remember? And I don't think you're easy. I don't even know you. But I want to. Know you, that is," he added darkly. "Is that a crime?"

Crime? No. Dream come true? Yes. Had any boy ever said something like that to me? Hell no. I lost my animosity, and a bubble of excitement expanded in my chest. He just, well, he sounded genuinely interested in me. Me!

The real you or the fake you? my mind chirped in. My excitement dimmed a little, and I gritted my teeth in annoyance. Thanks a lot, mind. It would have been nice to enjoy the moment.

I twisted the frayed fabric of my jeans between my fingers. "What about you? Are you dating anyone?"

"Nope." He paused, ran his bottom lip between his teeth. "Not yet."

O-kay. What did that mean? His husky tone suggested he

had someone in mind. Me? Probably. But I didn't have the courage to ask. I mean, this could be one of those moments where he wanted me to ask my friend if *she* liked him. In this case, that would mean he was interested in Avery. Gag.

I didn't like the girl enough to play her date pimp.

"We're here." He eased into a gravel lot and parked beside a white sedan. "I hope you're hungry."

As I exited, midday heat enveloped me. I hated how the weather could be freezing cold one day and blistering hot the next. Tomorrow it would probably rain. Or snow.

We walked side by side to the small, cozy brownstone situated between several other brownstones. Clarik was taller than me by several inches, and I felt tiny in comparison.

He opened the door for me, like we were on a real date. I gave him a half smile, swept past him—and froze.

Clarik bumped into my back, and I stumbled forward.

"What's wrong?" he asked.

"They're . . . they're . . ." I said, while inside I was screaming *no* at the top of my lungs.

"Yeah?"

Goth. Everyone was a fake Goth, just like at school. The waiters. The people eating. There was even a toddler draped in black crepe. Black, black, and more black, mixed with the occasional splash of blood-red. The lights were dimmed for atmosphere. The walls were mere shadows.

"We have to leave," I told Clarik, speaking past the sudden lump in my throat.

His hand settled on top of my shoulder. The heat of him soothed, but failed to comfort me completely. "Why?"

"I just, I have to leave, that's all." I didn't wait for his reply. I swung around and raced out the door, into the safety of the car. Was the entire world Goth? Would there be no safe haven from this sea of uniformity?

Expression somehow soft and hard at the same time, Clarik strode toward the car, his hands in his pockets. When he sat beside me, he jabbed the key into the ignition and said, "I'm not going to ask what that was about because I have a feeling you won't answer me."

"You're right."

"I'm starved, though. Is there any place you *will* eat?"

"Have you ever heard of Café Giovanni?"

"No."

I rattled off the address, hoping with all my heart it would be just as I remembered it. I could handle Goth there. It was expected. Familiar.

During the ten-minute drive, Clarik did his best to make me laugh by cracking jokes about all the different "Barbies" he'd encountered at Hell High. "Divorced Barbie a.k.a. Ms. Hamilton," he said, "comes with Ken's house, Ken's car, and Ken's entire wardrobe."

A twinge of amusement seeped past my upset. "I guess that means the Teen Barbie a.k.a. Mercedes will come with a back-stabbing knife," I said dryly.

He barked out a laugh, and the sound of it was somehow . . . enchanting. "We're here," he said, a little nervously. Did he expect me to run this time, too?

The car eased to a stop. We quickly exited, crossed the paved but crumbling parking lot, and descended the metal stairs. Once again, he pushed open the restaurant door and I swept past him.

"I hope this— No," I said on a gasp. My gaze circled the one place that used to welcome me with open arms. No, no, no. No!

It seemed this, my refuge, was to be denied me, too. Gone were the black walls and vampire posters. The familiarity I'd needed. Now the entire place resembled something out of *Seventeen.* Colorful walls with swirling designs. Pop music *bump, bumping* from speakers. A strobe light. Waitresses on Rollerblades.

Count was behind the bar. He wore a white button-up shirt and his hair was cut in a short buzz. He smiled at a customer, and I saw that his teeth were normal, not shaved to razor-sharp fangs. His gaze moved across the room and paused on me. He frowned.

"Take me home," I said softly to Clarik. "Please. Just take me home."

Life seriously sucked!

At home, I paced the length of my bedroom. Posters of dragons, dark fairies, and Enya hung on the walls and whizzed past me. Back and forth, back and forth. A black comforter edged in lace draped the bed. I'd saved my lunch money and bought it without my dad's permission, replacing the Disney one I'd had since childhood.

Clarik—who hadn't said another word after that last disaster—had dropped me off here and returned to school. He probably thought I was weird.

Yes. Life definitely sucked.

My dad was gone—I don't know where he was, he hadn't left a note—so I was alone. I'd left my key at school and had to ask the neighbor, who had a spare, to let me inside.

So here I was. Alone, like I'd wanted, but just as miserable as before.

A Sidekick that wasn't mine lay on my nightstand, and it rang continuously. I pounded on it for a few minutes. When that didn't shut it up, I drop-kicked it out the window.

Desperate to get back to real life, I searched through the phone book for Ms. Hamilton's home number and address. Of course, she wasn't listed. Neither was Dr. Laroque. I had no luck with Google, either.

I did find Mercedes's number and called her up. She was still at school, so I left a message on her machine, telling her to for sure pick me up later. We had to find the laboratory.

Left. Right. Left. I placed one foot in front of the other. Right. Left. Each of my walls was a different color: yellow, light blue, emerald, and violet. Every time I turned, I saw a blurring, different shade. And every time I passed my room's only window, I saw the Jetta that sat immobile in the driveway. I didn't want to wait for Mercedes. I wanted to drive around right now and search. But . . .

I couldn't force myself to get behind the wheel.

"Coward," I muttered to my reflection as I passed my full-length mirror. I stomped my boots into the plush brown carpet. Dr. Laroque and Ms. Hamilton, damn them, had reached into the deepest recesses of my subconscious, found the absolute worst way to punish me, and shoved it in my face on a silver platter. Conformity. Sameness. Lack of originality.

My mom had hated it, too. She hadn't been Goth or anything like that. She'd been Emma Leigh, an identical twin who'd wanted to make her own place in the world. She'd painted all the walls in our house a different color so none of them would look the same. Like my room. "Isn't this better?" she'd said. "Now we'll always know which is which."

I missed her so much.

Tears burned the rims of my eyes, and I quickly brushed them away. No time for an emotional breakdown. I needed a plan of action, and as I continued to stalk from one side of my room to the other, I outlined what I'd already done and what I needed to do: Talk to Mercedes—done. Look for Ms. Hamilton—in progress. Look for the devil's laboratory—tonight. Then . . . what? What if I couldn't find Hammy and the lab had been moved? What if—

No! I couldn't allow myself to think like that. I *would* find a way home. I had to. If I had to pay someone to cast a magic spell or bargain with the Devil himself, I would get home.

What about Clarik?

I bit my bottom lip. Sure, it'd be nice having his attention for a bit longer, but I'd rather have it as *me*. Unpopular, despised me. Not that he liked me now. Not anymore. I'd probably ruined that at lunch. "Moron," I muttered.

The rest, well, I could totally live without. No (real) friends. A dad who liked me for the wrong reasons. The counterfeit obsession of my peers.

Briiiiing.

Startled by the sudden noise, I jumped. *Briiiiing!* When my heartbeat stilled, I padded to my side table. *Briiiiing!* Caller ID said White, Linda. Ohmygod. Linnie! Hope sparked to life inside me. She'd called. She'd really called me. Maybe she didn't hate me like the others. I didn't know how she'd managed to retain her true memories when no one else had, and I didn't care.

She'd called!

Briiiiing! Grinning, I hurriedly picked up the receiver. "Hello."

For a long while, she didn't respond. Then she cleared her throat. "Can I, uh, speak with Jade?"

"You are. Thank God! Linnie, I'm so glad you called."

Another pause. Crackling static. "What are you doing home? You're supposed to be at school."

"I came home early. Listen, you have no idea how much I

need a friend right now. I've had the worst day ever." I sucked in a breath. "I need you to read your cards. Something's happened and I'm hoping they'll—"

"I was going to leave a message," she said, cutting me off, "but I guess we can do this live."

In that instant, my hope frayed at the edges. She sounded so formal and stiff, so determined. "Do what?" I said, my shoulders slumping. Please let her be my friend, I prayed.

"I don't like the way you treated my friends today."

My friends, she'd said. As in—you're not one of us, Jade Leigh. "I did nothing wrong. And how do you know how I treated them?" I asked sternly. "You weren't even at school."

"Robb called me and told me how you yelled at Mercedes in the hall. How you tried to turn her against him. He told me how you pretended to be in some virtual game at lunch." Her voice rose with the heat of her anger. "You'd better watch yourself. We're tired of your reign of terror and if you aren't careful someone is going to shove you off your pedestal."

"Linnie, will you listen to yourself? I haven't done anything wrong!"

She laughed bitterly. "God, you're amazing. You'll say anything and blame anyone to make yourself appear innocent."

"Name something I've done. Name one thing." What kind of fake memory had the doctor given her? I found myself wondering, again, if the people in this game were even real or merely figments meant to torment me. Like ghosts.

Unreal, phantoms. Apparitions my brain insisted were real, so therefore they became real to me.

"I can't believe I'm even talking to you," she ground out. "You want me to name something? Fine. How about the time you Photoshopped Erica's face on a porn star's body and pasted the pictures all over school?"

I gasped. "That wasn't me. That was Mercedes."

She snorted. "What about the time you poured juice over my head? Or the time you told Robb to pick you up and had your boyfriend waiting for him instead?" With every word she uttered, her upset grew. Once her voice even cracked, like she was fighting tears. "Shall I go on?"

Her words echoed in my head, and I suddenly felt like I was trapped in a small box, no air holes. Everything she'd named, Mercedes had done. Not me. Never me. I didn't know how to convince her of that, didn't know how to convince her of the truth. And that scared me. "Linnie, I never did those things."

"I suppose it was your other personality then. Or maybe the voices in your head made you do it."

"You don't understand. You're my friend, Linnie. My best friend. I would never do anything like that to you."

She snorted. "You're a bitch and a liar. I'd never—never!—be your friend."

"Linnie. Please. Listen to me. I—"

"Shut up. Shut the hell up."

"Linnie, please. Ask Mercedes." I'd said I wouldn't try and

explain to anyone else. Not again. But here I was, unable to stop myself and desperate to make her believe me. "She'll tell you. We're stuck in a game. I swear to God."

"That's funny, because she was laughing about you and your claim when I talked to her. Care to explain that?"

She laughed? Mercedes had laughed about the game? I scraped my nails over the surface of my desk. That bitch. "You have to remember—"

"Do me a favor. Go to hell." *Click.*

chapter eight

*What is the meaning of life? I think I
know the answer. Happiness. I think we're
all supposed to take our fair share of it
and help others find theirs—whether
that's in the light or the dark. When will
the rest of the world get the memo?*

disbelieving, I stared at the phone for a long while. She'd been so adamant in her hatred toward me, more so than the others. With that realization, horrible thoughts began to sweep through me. What if the virtual reality game had merely allowed Linnie's real feelings to surface? What then?

Had all my friends secretly hated me? I wondered, paranoid now.

For the first time in our entire six-year friendship, Linnie had hung up on me. She'd refused to listen, had defended Mercedes. Mercedes Turner of all people.

With a defeated breath, I replaced the phone in its cradle. I had no idea what to do about my friends, and I wasn't given a chance to think about it. I heard the front door swing open, heard my dad stroll inside the house, whistling under his breath. Great. I wasn't ready to deal with him and didn't want to explain why I'd ditched. There was no help for it, though. It had to be done.

"Dad," I called.

"Jade?" Surprise layered his voice.

I abandoned the safety of my room and strode into the hallway. He met me halfway, his expression dark with curiosity.

"Where were you?" I asked at the same time he said, "Why are you home from school?"

I racked my brain for a good reason, but nothing came to me. Finally I shrugged and opted for the truth. "I needed some alone time."

"Oh. Okay." Without another word, he turned and padded into the kitchen.

That's it? No, "You can't take a break from life, so why should you be allowed to take a break from school?" No, "Do you think you'll be able to ditch your job when you have a family to feed?"

Open mouthed, I followed the same path he had taken. "That's all you have to say to me?"

"Yes." He thumbed through the mail. "You're a smart girl, and I trust your judgment. If you needed a day off, you needed a day off."

"But, Dad. I ditched."

"I know, sweetie, but you had a good reason."

When I got over my shock, my mouth curled in a slow smile. Okay. So. There were now two things I liked about this Gothy otherworld. The way Clarik looked at me, and my dad's new and improved attitude about ditching. "Sweetie" didn't even bother me this time.

Those reasons weren't enough to make me want to stay in this reality, but. . . . They were oh so sweet, and I desperately needed a silver lining.

My dad cast me a quick glance and set the mail on the counter. "I've got to make a call, so . . ."

"So," I prompted.

"So. It's private."

I remained in place, watching him, studying his face. His lips pressed into a firm line, and I sighed. "Fine. I'll be in my room." I spun on my heel and tromped into the hall, then opened and closed my bedroom door—without going inside. I remained in the hall. He needed privacy? What for? He and I were not supposed to keep secrets from each other. That's what he'd once told me, at least.

I leaned against the cool wall, straining to listen. "We'll have to do it another day," I heard him say. Pause. "I'm sorry." Another pause. "I wanted to see you, too, but something's going on with Jade, and she really needs me right now."

Questions poured through my mind. Who had he planned to meet? A woman? Why was he so secretive about it? Was he dating someone special? In the two years since my mom's death, he'd only dated casually. Nothing serious. He'd never brought a woman home for me to meet, but I always knew when he scored (gag). He smiled for days afterward (double gag).

He ended the call, and I padded quietly into my room, shutting the door behind me with only the slightest snicker from the hinges.

I didn't like this new development.

The hours until nightfall dragged by, tortuous, one after the other. I stayed in my room the entire time. My dad even brought dinner to my door. I tried to write, but no words formed. Writing had always been my greatest refuge. Now, when I needed it most . . . I sighed in frustration and anger. I think, in that moment, I would have partied with Mr. Parton if it meant being able to write again.

With nothing else to do, I alternated between pacing and lying on the bed, staring up at the ceiling. Thinking, always thinking. No matter how many times I sorted through the questions about my dad, about the virtual reality game, about Clarik, about my friends, no answers were forthcoming. My dad's secret phone call—mystery. A way out of the game—mystery. Clarik's real thoughts about me—mystery. A way to convince my friends they really loved me—mystery.

And I freaking hated mysteries!

What the hell time was it now?

I glanced at the clock on my computer for the thousandth time and pushed out a relieved breath. Couldn't be much longer now. 11:05 P.M. Lying on the softness of the mattress, I stuffed my hands in my pockets and fingered my dad's pocketknife. I'd taken it. Just in case. I only prayed I *didn't* need to use it.

Moonlight slithered past my curtains, crimson mixed with gold. What time would Mercedes get here? Had she even gotten my message? I was going crazy waiting for her to pick me up so we could search for the lab.

And who would have thought I'd ever look forward to *her* presence?

A knock sounded at my door. I inwardly groaned and rolled my eyes. My dad had come in here four times already, only to be met with an inquisition and glaring. Never give up until you have the desired results, was his motto.

"What do you want now?" I called.

"It's a school night, sweetie. You should be in bed."

"I'm not tired."

Heavy pause. Then, "Are you decent?"

"Yes," I admitted reluctantly. Just go away! I thought. I wore army fatigues and a black shirt so I'd better blend into the night. I hope he didn't question me about it. Where was Mercedes?

My dad peeked his dark head past the door, expression somber, serious. "I want to talk to you."

"Fine. Let's start with where you were when I got home and who you canceled your secret plans with."

The question had driven him away the other four times. Not this time, though. Unfortunately. "That's not important," he said, coming into the room and easing onto the edge of the bed.

"If you want to talk about me, you're wasting your time. You have your secrets and I have mine," I said.

"Honey, I'm just trying to understand what's going on with you. I've never seen you behave this way."

My brows furrowed together. "What way?"

"So . . ." He spread his arms wide, encompassing me, my room. "So unpredictable."

"Dad, you wouldn't believe me if—"

A *clang clang* rattled my window, saving me from the rest of my reply. A part of me wanted to tell him the truth, wanted his help. The other part of me knew what would happen if I did. Disbelief. Drug testing. Maybe even laughter. No, I'd learned my lesson. Twice. I wasn't telling anyone else.

Clang. Clang.

I glanced at the glass. So did my dad. He frowned. "Is someone out there?" he asked, an ominous edge to the words.

I strode to the glass and glanced out, my shoulders slumping in relief. Thank God. "It's Mercedes."

"Mercedes Turner?" His frown deepened, pulling the skin

around his lips taut. "Does Sus— her mom know she's out this late?"

"Does it matter?" I signaled that I'd be out in a minute, and Mercedes nodded in understanding. She trekked back to her car, a pale slash in the moonlight.

My dad ignored my question—he was getting good at that. "You aren't hanging out with her, are you? She's not your usual type of friend."

"So?" I rushed to my closet and skimmed through my clothes, looking for my jacket.

"I don't want you around her, Jade," he said sternly. "She's trouble."

"I'll be fine."

Always the soldier, he tried another tactic. "This is a school night. You need to stay in."

"If you're worried I won't get enough sleep, don't. If I have to miss school tomorrow to catch up on my z's, I will. I know when I need a day off, remember?" I grabbed my purse and shoes.

"Jade . . ."

"You don't have to worry about my—what did you call it that day you gave me the sex talk?—flower, either. Mercedes will keep her hands to herself."

"That's not funny." Eyes slitted, he crossed his arms over his chest. "I don't want you going out this late at night. Dangerous people are out there, on the prowl for innocent young girls."

"We'll be careful. Promise. You know I love the night."

He pinched the bridge of his nose. "You're staying here, young lady, and that's final."

"I can't. I'm sorry. I have to go." I hated pissing him off, I really did. He wasn't a bad guy. However, I soothed myself with the thought that Mercedes and I would find the lab and the computers and whisk ourselves out of the game. Tomorrow my dad wouldn't remember that I'd disobeyed him.

"I want you to stay home," he said, using his toughest "dad voice." "I'm not asking. I'm telling."

"I'll see you later. Don't wait up." I kissed his cheek and raced out of my room, out of the house.

"Jade," he called, incredulous.

Cool night air brushed my face, and the car's bright lights made me squint. I loved this time of night. Shadows danced freely, and stars winked from a perch of black velvet. Insects hummed lazily.

"Jade, get back here," my dad shouted.

Heart racing, I slid into the blue sedan. I'd never been so blatant in my disobedience. "Floor it," I commanded Mercedes.

She did. Tires squealed and rocks flew from the back tires as we backed up and onto the road. We sped away. My stomach clenched, and I closed my eyes. My dad and his anger were forgotten, replaced by my fear of fast cars.

"What took you so long?" she demanded. "I had to wait for, like, ever."

"You waited two minutes. What took *you* so long to come get me?"

"Your dumb friends kept calling me. They even came over to my house."

Jealousy sparked to instant life. She dismissed them casually, while I would have done anything to have them like me again. "They aren't dumb. Got it?"

"Whatever." Finally, when we were a safe distance away, Mercedes slowed down.

I glared over at her. "Why did you laugh when Erica and Robb told you I'd told them about the game? Why did you laugh about it to Linnie?"

"I didn't know what else to say, all right? They were laughing about you and I didn't want them to laugh at me, too. Besides, I thought we agreed not to tell anyone." She shot me a frown.

I didn't reply.

"Think your dad will come looking for us?" she asked.

"No."

"My dad would have chased after me."

There was a defensive edge to her voice this time. "I thought he'd taken off a few years ago," I said.

She popped her jaw, but offered no response.

I cast a glance in her direction, and shook my head in puzzlement. She was dressed in a light green tank top (with lace) and a miniskirt (with lace at the hem). Green high heels were anchored to her feet and laced up her calves. "That's what you're wearing? Seriously? What if we have to break in?"

"Here's a free fashion tip: there's nothing wrong with looking good, no matter the circumstances." She gave me a brief once-over. "You really need to consider that."

My jaw clenched. There was nothing wrong with my clothes and nothing wrong with my appearance. If we *did* have to do a little B and E, I could climb, run, and move without restriction. She'd fall on her face. Amusing, yes, but it wouldn't get us home.

"So . . ." she said. Her fingers tightened on the steering wheel until her knuckles turned white. "Has Avery said anything about me?"

"No." Nothing good, that is. I didn't have to ask if Linnie and Erica had said anything about me. She'd already admitted they'd been laughing about me.

"What if we can't get home, Jade?" she asked suddenly. There was a raw quality to her voice I'd never heard from her before.

"We will." We had to.

"You say that so confidently." She sounded stronger, more like her normal self with every word. "What do you think? We'll find the lab, and *boom*—everything will be the same as it was?"

I traced a finger across the dusty window, leaving a line. "Maybe." I could hope, at least.

"Do you even remember where the lab is?" Frowning, she tunneled a hand through her pale hair. The car eased to a stop at a forked intersection, and she looked left, then right.

"Kind of," I hedged.

"Kind of?" She pinned me with a glare. "That doesn't help at all."

"I don't know the exact address. You don't either, so zip it. You're heading in the right direction, though. North on Western."

She eased the car left, mumbling, "Let's hope we know it when we see it."

One hour, three wrong turns and multiple shouting matches later, we found it. Excitement thrummed through me when I spotted the tall, brown brick building, still crumbling and covered in graffiti. There were no cars in the lot tonight. No lights or lampposts to illuminate the area.

For once, I didn't like the dark.

Mercedes parked in front and gazed at the building with trepidation. "It's creepy. I don't remember it looking *this* creepy."

I agreed. I knew what was inside, had experienced terror in there, and did not look forward to a repeat experience. Just being here, I felt exposed and vulnerable.

Mercedes cut the engine, and total silence blanketed us. She switched off the car lights, and total darkness consumed us. Every horror movie I'd ever watched played through my mind. I gulped.

"Should we, like, go in?" All hint of superiority had washed from her tone. She oozed fear.

"Yes?" I'd meant the word as a statement, but it emerged as a question.

"Okay," she said.

"Okay," I repeated.

Neither of us moved. I think a little demon had taken residence inside my chest and was using my heart for drum practice. I'd brought my dad's pocketknife, but all of a sudden it didn't seem like enough protection.

"I brought my Sidekick," she said. "Maybe we should call someone. Or e-mail the police so they can read it after they find our dead, bloody bodies and know where to start looking for our killer."

"We need inside that building, and I doubt the police will help us do that. We can do this ourselves." I drew in a deep breath, forced my hand on the car door handle, and opened the door. A cool breeze wafted inside, scented with . . . danger? The small hairs on the back of my neck stood at attention, and I felt a pair of eyes boring into me. Watching.

My blood chilled.

"What if people are inside?" she whispered.

I gulped down the lump that had beaded in my throat. "They aren't," I forced myself to say. *I'm not being watched, I'm not being watched.*

"How can you be so sure? They could be inside, waiting for us. Maybe they wanted us to come so they could put us inside another game. A *worse* game."

I gripped the edge of the door, unable to tear my eyes

from the building. Stay strong. Stay calm. We were alone, I assured myself, the only people in the vicinity. "You're hysterical, Mercedes. Do I need to slap you?"

She inhaled sharply, then exhaled a shaky, unsteady puff of air. "You're such a bitch. You know that?"

"It's sweet of you to notice," I said with a false, sugar-sweet tone.

"So what are you waiting for?" She flipped her hair over her shoulder. "An engraved invitation? Get the rest of the way out, shut the car door, and go inside."

I flashed her a scowl and stood. Another breeze trickled past, the night air coiling around me. It did little to soothe the nervous sweat pearling on my skin.

Mercedes remained in her seat. She looked from me to the building, the building to me. "I'll wait here and keep the car running. That way, we can make a fast getaway if we need to."

Yeah, like I'd really leave her out here to drive away without me. Since my door was still open, I leaned into the car, grabbed the keys from the ignition, and stuffed them into my pocket.

She gasped. "Give those back."

"Come and get them." I slammed my car door shut. The loud thump echoed in my ears, and I cringed. I scanned the parking lot nervously, still feeling that invisible gaze on me and halfway expecting someone to jump from the shadows, screaming, "Boo!"

Just your imagination, Jade, I told myself.

"Fine." Mercedes exited and stomped to the trunk. She raised it and dug inside, withdrawing two flashlights. "Here." She tossed one at me.

I barely managed to catch it. "Thanks." I hadn't expected her to do something so intelligent—or considerate, since she'd brought two. I guess even festering wounds that plagued humanity could have moments of greatness.

Gravel crunched as she closed the distance between us until she finally stood at my side. I noticed she was shaking, her entire body radiating plumes of fear. Did mine?

I raised my chin. "Let's do this."

Inch by torturous inch, we approached the building (a.k.a. hell). The front door, of course, was locked, as were the two closest windows. One, of which, was boarded.

"We'll have to break the glass." Nibbling on my lip, I peeked inside. Only darkness greeted me, so much thicker and more oppressive than the darkness outside.

"What if we set off an alarm?" she whispered.

"We run like hell, hide and wait."

"But—"

"It's a chance we have to take." We were here, and no one had jumped us. We weren't leaving until we'd searched every inch of the building. I bent down, flashing my light over the flower bed as I rummaged for a large rock. "We're getting inside *tonight.* No matter what."

She swallowed audibly and crouched beside me. "Just so

you know," she said without heat, "when this is over we are so not friends."

"I'm glad we're on the same page." Bitch. "You do realize you're the reason there are drug addicts at our school, right? People will do anything to escape the reality of you."

She drew in a sharp—dare I say hurt?—breath, and I felt a rush of guilt. "Your jealousy is showing," she snapped.

"I'm not jealous of you." I popped my jaw, trying to tamp down my anger. All sense of guilt abandoned me. "I pity you."

"Ha! You liked Bobby Richards, but he didn't want you. You liked Clarik—and don't try to deny it because I saw the way you were looking at him—but he didn't like you back, either. Both of them wanted me. *Me.*"

"Not anymore they don't." My fingers curled around a medium-size, jagged rock. I hefted it in my palm and stood. I ground my teeth together and bit the inside of my cheek until I drew blood. Hearing those words—"he didn't like you back"—stung. Hard core.

"Like that means anything," she muttered. "You know they don't like the real you."

"I'm the same girl I was before," I replied, even though I'd thought those very words myself.

"They like your popularity. Your *fake* popularity."

She always knew the exact thing to say to wound me.

Without another word, I launched the rock at the window. Glass shattered, raining and tinkling onto the ground. I stood, waiting, locked in place. Ready to run. Thankfully, no alarm erupted.

"Give me some warning next time," Mercedes grumbled. She tossed her flashlight through the opening, illuminating the room in a golden glow.

I did the same. "Hopefully there won't be a next time."

"Whatever. Give me a boost."

I bent my knees and locked my hands together, and she used me as a spring, climbing easily inside. Her high heel dug into my skin, and I grimaced. Surprisingly, she leaned out and offered me a hand, pulling me up.

"Thank you," I forced myself to say.

We each grabbed a flashlight, but neither of us moved forward. We shined our lights over our surroundings. Disappointment. Regret. Anger. I experienced all three.

"It's empty," Mercedes said on a moan. "Everything is the same—the walls, the room, but no equipment!"

"This is only one office." I had to stay positive or I'd do something stupid. Like cry. "It doesn't mean anything."

"What if—"

"Don't say it. Don't even think it. The equipment has to be here. Somewhere." My words echoed off the bare walls, hopeful, desperate.

Clutching the light in an iron fist, I kicked at the locked door, once, twice. I had no luck, so Mercedes joined in. On our third kick, wood splintered from the hinges and opened up into another room. We looked at each other, then held our flashlights forward.

Empty.

My stomach twisted painfully.

"Jade," she said, her voice shaky.

"I know," I replied, just as shaky. Just as upset. We explored the place from top to bottom. Papers were scattered across the floor, but that was it. Nothing else. I glanced over them, seeing only gibberish. Numbers, symbols, letters. I stuffed as many of the papers as I could into my pockets. But . . .

It wasn't what I'd hoped for.

Where were the computers? The machines? I swung around, shaking my head in disbelief. In horror.

"How did they move the equipment so quickly?" Mercedes shouted. She was no longer trying to be quiet. "They took everything!"

"They couldn't have moved it far. We'll find it."

"How?" she demanded.

"I don't know." I crisscrossed my arms over my middle, my gaze still searching as I tamped down my panic.

"We're stuck here," she said, voicing my fears. "Just say it. We're stuck in this hellish nightmare of a reality."

"If there's a way in, there's a way out. We'll talk with Ms. Hamilton." Even to my own ears, the words were lame.

"Do you really expect her to help us? Tell me you're not that stupid, Jade. She's the one who signed us up for this. She's probably left the country by now. Who knows? She might not even be part of the game."

I couldn't accept defeat. I couldn't accept what had been done to us without a fight. There had to be another way out.

"She *is* part of the game. Everyone still knows her at school. We *will* find her and force her to help us."

Mercedes laughed that bitter laugh of hers. "The chances of finding her are about as good as us finding the computers in this empty building."

"She has to show up sometime," I said, determined.

"Why? We don't know how the game works. This isn't real life. She might know everything we plan. She might be able to come in and out at will, always staying a step ahead of us."

My stomach rolled at the thought.

"We're stuck here," she repeated. "Stuck like this." Her hand waved to me, then over herself. "Stuck with you as the darling of the school, and me as an outcast. A freak." Her voice broke and tears streamed down her eyes, streaking her perfect makeup. "You're the freak, not me."

"Okay. That's it." I closed the small distance between us, putting us nose-to-nose—a familiar position for us. Place us in the same room and we were like animals fighting over territory, I guess. We forgot about our situation, forgot why we were there, and allowed the past to consume us. "Stop calling me names. Do you hear me? Stop it. You've done it for years and I'm sick of it!"

"Get out of my face." She pushed me.

I stumbled backward, righted myself, then pushed her back. "I want to get home just as much as you do."

"You're adored here. I wouldn't doubt if you warned Dr. Laroque we were coming so he could move the equipment."

I gasped. "I never warned him."

"You love it here, admit it."

"I'm adored, yes, but I'm also a clone. One of the crowd, and there's nothing that sets me apart."

"So," she spat.

So? I glared at her, incredulous. She really didn't get it.

"You're not a freak now. You can't tell me you liked that."

"I didn't, no. I hate being called a freak, but I'd rather be a freak than invisible. When you blend into the crowd, Mercedes, you're nothing special. You're one of a thousand others. You have no real value."

"Uh, I hate to break it to you, but *you* blend with *your* friends. You all love weird, stupid things. And hello, you don't have to be different to be special." She shook her head. "Who fed you that line of crap?"

I shoved her again, harder this time, and she fell back with a gasp, tripping on her heels. She stayed down, glowering at me. "Do you know what my mom's last words were to me?" I growled. "Our car had flipped and stayed upside down. Her blood was dripping on me as she died and do you know what her last words were? Do you?" I was screaming toward the end, but couldn't stop myself.

"No," Mercedes croaked.

I knew the words by heart. I'd memorized them, replayed them a thousand times. "'There are two kinds of people,' she'd said. 'Those who coast through life like ducks in a row, following one after the other, and those who ride the waves.'"

Tears spilled down my cheeks, and my voice cracked. "'Ride the waves, baby, and live. Live.'"

Silence.

"I choose to live, Mercedes. Okay? I choose to be me, to be different than everyone else. To stand out. When she looks down at me, she'll know exactly who I am. Do you understand now? Do you get it?"

"Jade," Mercedes began, but whatever else she was going to say was cut off when red-and-blue lights flashed through the windows, almost like a strobe.

My focus whipped to the side. So did hers.

"Come out with your hands up," a deep, male voice commanded.

chapter nine

*I think the great Captain Kirk once
said, "Why can't we all just get along?"
Wait. Maybe that was Tiny Tim.
Either way, it seems like an impossible
dream.*

risked, cuffed, and helped into a police car.

Sound fun? Exciting? Adventurous? It's not.

They confiscated the papers I'd stuffed into my pockets, and even took my pocketknife.

"Dr. Laroque hooked us to a computer and now we're inside a virtual reality game," Mercedes blurted out as she was shoved in beside me. "We just want to go home."

Several policemen laughed. I glared at her, silently commanding her to close her freaking mouth. All her words would get us was a psych exam.

"I'm serious," she whimpered.

"No, you're begging to be tested for drug use," one of the cops said. "Now shut up."

Thankfully she did.

We were driven downtown, and neither of us spoke a word to the other. My emotions were still too raw. Maybe hers were, too. One of the officers informed us that we'd tripped a silent alarm when we busted the window and the owner—Dr. John Laroque—had called them.

We hadn't been read our rights or anything like that, and weren't actually being arrested. We were being taken in so our parents could be notified. The owner, apparently, declined to press charges—the first and only nice thing Dr. Laroque had done for us. I could only hope guilt was eating him alive like a flesh-eating bacteria.

Would nothing go right today?

At the bustling station, I noticed the criminals being booked and processed were dressed liked Barbie clones, wearing conservative pastels and tidy button-downs and slacks. The male police officers, I realized in the light, wore black eyeliner and sported multiple tattoos.

The switch was startling.

Mercedes and I were locked in a small, bland room that offered nothing more than thick, musky air, a scarred table, and a few unpadded chairs. We were escorted to opposite ends of the table and uncuffed.

Leaning back, I stretched out my legs and sighed. The officers left us then, one of them muttering, "Be good. We'll be watching from the two-way."

"This is all *your* fault," Mercedes said the moment the door closed.

My mouth opened and closed with a snap. "My fault?"

"You're bad luck, obviously."

"Ever stop and consider the possibility that *you* might be the bad luck charm in this relationship?"

Her eyes narrowed to tiny slits. "You could have helped me out and told them what happened to us."

"Like you helped me with my friends? They could have locked us both away, Mercedes. What then, huh?"

Mutinous, she turned away from me and faced the wall.

The clock ticked away the ensuing hour of silence. I shifted uncomfortably in my seat a thousand times, my nerves so frayed they threatened to break apart at any moment. I was thirsty, tired, stressed, disappointed, and frustrated. Not a good combination.

Where was my dad?

Finally, hinges squeaked as the door glided open. A policeman I didn't recognize stepped inside. He had bright, bottle-red hair, and white doughnut powder around his mouth. Some things never changed, I guess.

"Your parents are here, girls." He dripped with disapproval, as if we should have been left here to rot. "They'd like to talk to you."

Mercedes paled. I'm sure I did, too. My dad was going to

kill me. There'd be none of this "pick your own punishment" or "no TV for you" this time around, even as nice as he'd been lately.

The officer stepped aside, and my dad strode past him. Susan, Mercedes's mom, followed on his heels. Her hair— Impossible! She was Goth. She'd dyed her hair black. It was a tangled mess with vivid green streaks interwoven throughout. Her black, hooker-style dress was wrinkled. Lines of anger and tension bracketed her fake green eyelashes and around her mouth.

My dad looked just as disheveled. His shirt was untucked, and he wore brown house loafers.

"Are you okay?" he asked me, his voice deep with concern.

The concern surprised me a little. Last time I'd seen him, he'd been pissed at me. "I'm fine."

"Thank God," he said, and breathed a sigh of relief.

His footsteps thudded as he closed the rest of the distance between us. He curved a hand over my shoulder and squeezed. "They called me, and . . ." A shudder worked through him. "I haven't stopped worrying since."

Susan crossed her arms over her chest and glared down at Mercedes. "How could you do this? Tell me how you could blithely break the law, deface someone else's property, then lie about being trapped in some stupid game."

Remaining silent, Mercedes turned away from her.

"Do you realize what a bad influence you are to your sister? She looks up to you."

"I never lied," Mercedes said softly.

Susan laughed bitterly, a perfect mimic of Mercedes's laughter earlier. "I'm not stupid, but I am fed up." She turned to my dad; their eyes met for the briefest of seconds. "This behavior ends now."

My breath snagged hot and shallow in my throat. It was the same kind of "look" Linnie and Robb had shared the day before I entered the game—or had years passed? It felt like an eternity had inched by unnoticed. Only this look was more heated, more intense, and filled with longing.

I wanted to deny it, to pretend I hadn't seen it.

"I'm sorry, Blake," Susan said. "My daughter got yours involved in this, and that's unforgivable. Mercedes has always been trouble, but to bring your innocent little girl down with her . . ."

Mercedes's mouth fell open. "What?"

I blinked in shock. "Yeah. What?"

"I'm sorry, too," my dad replied, ignoring us, concentrating only on Susan. "I thought they hated each other, and I always regretted that fact. Until now. I think I'd prefer hatred to"—his hand swept over us—"this."

"I'll punish her," Susan assured him. "Mercedes *will* regret this."

They were casting all the blame on Mercedes; they saw me as the innocent. Inconceivable!

"Do you not love me anymore?" Mercedes asked softly. She faced her mom, a tear rolling down her cheek.

"I love you," Susan said, her features crumbling. She took a step toward Mercedes, then stopped herself. She straightened her shoulders and squared her chin. "I love you, but I cannot tolerate your behavior anymore."

Mercedes pounded a fist against the table surface, and the force of it vibrated all the way to me. "I haven't done anything wrong."

"You broke into a building and dragged poor Jade with you."

"Well," I began. I wasn't going to pretend to be guiltless in this. I'd own up to my part in it. "Mercedes didn't drag me along. I asked her to pick me up and—"

"Hush, Jade," my dad said. "Mercedes picked *you* up. *She* drove to the building. We all know who's at fault here."

"Yes." Looking utterly exhausted, Susan scrubbed a hand down her face, smearing her mascara. "Don't try to defend her."

"Dad, do you not remember the way I ran out of the house? Do you not remember how I disobeyed your orders to stay home?"

Mercedes wiped angrily at her tears, sweeping them away. Her chin lifted defiantly, and for a moment she resembled her mom. "All you care about anymore is *him*." "Him," apparently, was my dad. She spat the word and glared. "You kicked Daddy out for him. You destroyed my life for him. All I did was break into a stupid building—and I had a good reason. You broke Daddy's heart. You broke my heart. All because you're the most selfish person in the world."

With Mercedes's words, the small, airless box I'd encountered earlier closed around me again, suffocating me. "Dad?" I managed to push the word past my constricted throat.

He coughed. "We'll talk about it later, Jade."

I stared up at him, at his guilty expression, and I knew, *knew*, he and Susan were more than friends. "How long?" I gritted out.

Silence. Heavy, gut-wrenching silence.

"How long!" In a perfect mimic of Mercedes, I banged my fist into the table.

"Years." Mercedes spoke to me, but glared at her mom. "Two years."

Two years. And I hadn't known. Hadn't suspected. He'd hid Susan from me like a dirty secret. "We'll always be honest with each other," he'd once told me. Yeah. Sure. What that meant was that I needed to spill all my secrets while he kept his safely tucked away.

I'd never felt so betrayed.

"Jade," he began.

"No," I said, choking back my anger, my tears. "Don't." I wish I could delude myself and pretend this was just part of the game. It wasn't. Mercedes had known before the game and, like me, her mind hadn't been altered. She had the same memories she'd had before.

"Okay, folks." The policeman scratched the side of his face and adjusted his belt; he appeared uncomfortable listening to our family squabble. "Let's wrap this up."

Susan sighed heavily. "I'm sorry you found out this way, Jade."

"Can we go now?" I asked the officer, ignoring her. I didn't glance in my dad's direction, either.

"Yes."

My dad gently gripped my upper arm and helped me to my feet. "I'll take you home, honey. Susan," he added with a nod. He paused. "I'll call you in the morning."

She nodded in return and looked away guiltily.

I was tugged from the room, but my gaze remained locked on Susan the entire time as questions raced through my mind. Had she "dated" my dad before my mom's death?

Had my mom known?

Neither my dad nor I spoke a word as we strode out of the station and into our car. He keyed the engine. Puffs of cool air leaked from the vents, and a golden oldie rocked softly from the speakers.

"Susan and I—" he began.

"Don't," I said, stopping him. I was too frayed, too raw. "Just don't." I stared out the window, at the stars winking in the black sky.

"I have to."

"No. You 'had to' years ago. Now it's too late."

"I didn't know how to tell you. You were so close to your mom and devastated by her death."

My hands fisted on my pants, twisting the material. I didn't want to hear this. "And you weren't? I remember the way you cried for her. Was that a lie?"

He leaned his forehead against the wheel. "I didn't want you to think I was replacing her. I would never have . . ."

I squeezed my eyelids tightly closed and blocked out his voice. You know what's funny in a horrible, twisted way? Dr. Laroque and Ms. Hamilton thought they'd have to put me inside a VR game to take away my identity, to teach me a lesson, and make me appreciate the life I used to have.

They didn't have to.

All they would have had to do was tell me about my dad and Mercedes's mom.

chapter ten

Boys are from Mars.

"**b**reakfast is ready," my dad called, his voice seeping past my closed bedroom door.

Eyes squeezed tightly shut, I groaned and rolled over in my bed. Sunlight shoved past my curtains, bright, unwelcome, and unwanted. "Go away," I croaked. "Want to sleep more."

"Up and at 'em."

"Noooo."

"Yes."

I'd tossed and turned all night and finally cried myself to sleep. Now my eyelids felt heavy, my eyes burned, and my chest ached. Maybe if I slept for an eternity, I'd wake up rested.

"Get up, Jade, before I throw ice water in your face."

He'd do it, too; he'd done it before. I slammed a fist into the soft pillow and eased up, blinking open my tired eyes. My mouth stretched wide in a yawn, and I arched my spine. My hair tumbled down my back, tickling.

"You getting up?" he demanded.

I tossed my pillow at the door.

He chuckled, and the sound of his amusement had me gritting my teeth. No one should be so happy in the morning—especially him. Not after last night.

I hurried through a shower, then stood in my closet, staring at the sea of black clothes. Whatever I wore, I'd look exactly like a thousand other people.

Sighing, I dragged out a pair of tight black pants. I anchored a thick, glittery silver belt around my waist. If I'd owned a white dress, I would have worn it. Instead I ended up wearing a black puff-sleeved top with silver veins running through it. I brushed my hair and left it hanging down my back.

At the kitchen table, my dad was shoveling two plates high with eggs, bacon, and toast. He spotted me and smiled. "You look pretty."

Don't smile at me, I almost snapped. "I look exhausted."

Slowly his grin faded. He slid a plate in front of me, set one at his side of the table, and eased into his chair. "Listen, about yesterday—"

"Forget it." I spooned a bite of too-salted eggs into my mouth.

"I should have told you about Susan. I admit that. I was wrong. But I want you to like her, Jade. I—I love her."

I swallowed, the eggs dropping like lead in my stomach.

"You'll understand one day," he continued. "Love isn't something you can fight or control. It just happens, and you're helpless."

Stop, I almost shouted. "Were you . . . dating her before mom died?"

"No," he said firmly.

I pushed my eggs with my fork, scooting them from one side of the plate to the other. "Why keep her a secret then? If you love her like you say, why hide her from your only child?"

"I didn't think you were ready to accept another woman in my life."

"You didn't give me a chance, did you?"

His cheeks colored slightly. Score one for me. Too bad it was a bittersweet victory and didn't make me any happier. "Look," I said, standing, "I've got to go."

He stood, too. "I'll drive you."

"No thanks. I'll walk."

Since I'd left my bag and books at school, I had nothing to carry. I stuffed my hands in my pockets and, without another word, strolled outside. Just as I stepped onto the porch and a breeze of cool, fragrant air caressed me, a hearse pulled into the driveway. I blinked in surprise, not knowing what to expect.

Bobby unfolded from the driver's seat, Avery from the

passenger's side. So not their usual car. She grinned and waved me over. "I tried to call and e-mail—again—but you haven't responded. Anyway, I heard you walked to school yesterday and didn't want you to have to do it again. Come on, let's go!"

Behind me, my dad's footsteps echoed. "I want to drive you, sweetie, so we can continue our talk."

I didn't turn around, didn't respond in any way. Dread swimming through me, I raced to the hearse and jumped into the back. I cast a glance toward the porch. My dad was frowning, his eyes a little sad. Car keys dangled from his fingers.

My throat constricted. "Drive," I commanded Bobby.

The car sped into motion and soon (thankfully) my dad was out of view entirely. When he'd said that he loved Susan, I'd felt the words cut me all the way to the bone. The woman had replaced my mom in his heart. How unfair. And wrong. She wasn't good enough for him!

"Why haven't you answered your Sidekick?" Avery asked me.

I bit my lip and shrugged. "I lost it?" The words emerged as more a question than a statement.

"Oh," she said, disappointed.

"So, Jade," Bobby said, breaking into my thoughts, "I heard you were hanging with Mercedes Turner last night. What's that about? First you defend her in class, then you willingly spend time with her."

"Yeah." Avery smoothed back her hair and anchored the

dark, dyed strands in a twisted ponytail. "She's such a loser. Aren't you afraid you'll be tainted by her?"

How could I respond to that? What could I say that wouldn't have them asking me ten million other questions?

"Well?" Avery prompted. "You haven't been yourself lately. What's going on with you?"

"What, are you guys my parents now and I have to explain myself to you?"

"No." Bobby waggled his eyebrows. "But I'd be your daddy if you asked me real nice."

Avery snorted and slapped him in the arm. "You're such a perv." She turned back to me. "She called me yesterday, you know, and said we were best friends and you were a fake." Avery made a gagging noise. "As if."

"She called you?" I asked, and Avery nodded.

"I think she's on serious drugs," Bobby said.

"I heard her dad shacked up with a senior from Capital Hill. How gross is that?"

Bobby shrugged. "Her mom is fiiiine, though. Smokin'. I'd tap her, no doubt about it."

Avery slapped his arm again. "You want to tap every ass you see."

"Ow! Nothing wrong with looking. Jade knows I would never touch."

Again, Avery snorted.

I watched the exchange with fascination. They were relaxed, completely at ease, and made sure to include me by casting me conspiratorial glances. I found it was oddly comforting. And realizing I was comforted by Bobby and Avery made me feel guilty, like I was betraying Erica, Linnie, and Robb. I sighed. Would I never feel sane and unconflicted again?

"Looks like John Hodges wants to race me," Bobby said. He hit the gas and we revved into high speed.

Breath caught in my throat, and my heart thumped like a rock band's drums. "Slow down!" We were close to the school and kids were on the sidewalks.

Bobby laughed. "I own, man, I own! He'll never catch us. I've got mad skills behind the wheel."

"Slow down," I said, with more force this time. I squeezed my eyes closed so I wouldn't have to see the trees and people whizzing past us.

When we reached the school, Bobby slowed down (thank God!) and parked as close to the front door as possible—actually taking a handicapped space, which was widely known as "Bobby's spot." No one dared chastise him for fear he'd beat the crap out of them. Even Ms. Hamilton let him park there, the hypocrite.

Why wasn't *he* being taught a lesson?

"We seriously need to teach that Barbie freak a lesson," Avery said.

Hearing her mirror my own thoughts gave me pause. "Just leave her alone," I said. But there was a sweet kind of justice in the thought of Avery going after Mercedes. The problem was, both Mercedes and I were in the process of learning Dr. Laroque and Ms. Hamilton's miserable lesson. We didn't need instructing from anyone.

Avery shrugged and hefted her black velvet bag onto her shoulder. She emerged from the car, a fairy goddess bestowing her presence on her subjects. She looked amazing today. She had bleached several stripes of her hair white so they made a startling contrast against the black locks. She wore a frayed mini and multicolored suspenders that mimicked wings.

I would have loved the outfit on anyone else.

Uttering another sigh, I stepped outside and into the bright, slightly cool morning. My legs were a little shaky. Bobby raced off to gloat over John. Goth kids were everywhere. Some loitered in the yard, talking, some entered the building, ready to start their days.

Welcome to hell, I thought.

Ms. Hamilton didn't show up that day. In fact, the vice principal announced Hammy was sick and wouldn't be returning for a while. I knew the diabolical woman wasn't sick (except in the head). She was simply too much of a coward to face me and Mercedes.

Silver lining: class elections were pushed back until her return. At least I wouldn't have to deal with life as president. Another silver lining: Avery and the others weren't all that bad. Every time they saw me in the halls, they squealed happily. They seemed to really enjoy talking to me; they listened to me. They *included* me.

I'd hated that very thing yesterday. For some reason, it didn't bother me today. Maybe the shock of the reality switch had worn off. I don't know. I'd just, well, I'd been picked on for so long, it was nice to be accepted for a change—even though I knew, deep down, it was wrong.

When school let out, I didn't even mind when Avery air kissed me good-bye. I used to gag when she and Mercedes did that, but stupid me, I kind of liked it when *I* was involved. "Are you going to the Coffin Club meeting?"

I wrinkled my nose. What was the Coffin Club? Wait, maybe I didn't want to know. "No."

"Oh." She sighed in disappointed. "Do you want a ride home?"

A group of boys on skateboards flew past us. "Nah," I said. "I'll be fine."

"See you tomorrow then," she said. "Call me later, 'k? Love ya."

"Love . . . ya," I returned, frowning. I didn't even say that to Erica and Linnie. Not that they said it to me.

Pensive, I kicked into motion and headed toward my locker. I rounded the corner, only to see Clarik scowling and pointing a finger in a pale, shaking boy's face. "You don't yell at girls. Do you understand me?"

"I'm sorry. I didn't mean anything by it."

"What's going on?" I asked, looking around at the growing crowd.

Clarik spun around, facing me. The boy used the distraction to his advantage and raced away. "I didn't like the way he was treating his girlfriend, that's all." His eyes were bright with fury. He walked toward me without another word and reached into his pocket. When he passed me, he didn't pause, didn't slow, just withdrew his hand, jabbed a note into mine, and kept walking.

I stopped, staring down at it in confusion. After unfolding it (with shaky hands), I read: Meet me at the football field.

Meet him. *Me.* I nearly kissed the paper before I stuffed it into my pocket. Why? I wondered. What did he want? Eager, I didn't waste time gathering my books—why bother with homework when this wasn't the real world—I skipped to the field and leaned against the black-and-red concession stand wall. There weren't many boys practicing because football was no longer fright.

No sign of Clarik yet.

Several minutes passed, but he didn't arrive. Where was he? Maybe he was playing a joke on me and wasn't going to show up. I felt the color drain from my face. I would not wait around for that. I stepped toward the field, meaning to walk home, when I spied Mercedes, Erica, and Linnie ambling onto the sidelines. I froze in place.

Erica and Linnie were wearing short shorts and sports bras, and began jumping up and down and yelling, "Go team!" Mercedes was instructing them on . . . cheerleading? Seriously?

"Keep your legs straight." Pause. "Good. Perfect."

They ate up her every word as if she were giving them instructions on how to cheat on their SAT exams without getting caught.

Hidden as I was by the thick walls, they hadn't noticed me yet. I blatantly watched and listened. And yes, I was jealous about the easy camaraderie they shared. That should be *me* instructing them. Not that I knew anything about cheerleading. Not that I ever planned to learn. Still.

"Your wrists are broken," Mercedes said. "You have to keep your arms straight. Like this." She held her arms over her head in a V. "See?"

Both girls nodded and mimicked the action.

"Good," she praised. "You've got it." With barely a breath, she asked, "So where's Stilts—I mean, that tall boy? The one who's always hanging around with you? Robin? I thought he'd be here, watching."

Linnie rolled her eyes and dropped her arms to her side. "You know his name. You know our names, too, and I wish to God you'd stop pretending you don't. The joke is getting old."

"*Robb* is at home," Erica said, flopping down on the green grass. Sweat glistened on her pale skin. "He thinks you hate him."

A look of guilt flashed over Mercedes face. "Just call him and tell him I'm sorry for yelling at him, all right? I'm just, well, I don't want to date anyone right now."

"You're breaking up with him?" Linnie asked. There was no anger in her tone. She glanced down at her shoes and kicked a rock. "For real?"

"We never really dated," Mercedes said, exasperated. "Forget I brought him up. I don't want to talk about him anymore. We need to buy you guys Sidekicks. That way, you can call, e-mail, and text me with the latest gossip. Aver— never mind. Just plan on buying one soon, okay?"

"No way. That's so conformist. I hear the Goth clones use those." Erica rolled to her side and stared over at Mercedes. "Hey, shouldn't you be at home? You're grounded."

"Like my mom can really force me to stay home if I don't want to be there."

Linnie smoothed her hand over her short brown bob. "What's with you hanging out with Jade Leigh, anyway? I thought you hated her as much as we do. She's—"

"Hey," Clarik said.

Yelping, I whipped around to face him. "Clarik," I said, a hint of guilt in my voice. Caught spying. How embarrassing. Had the girls heard me?

He laughed, his blue eyes twinkling. "Sorry. I didn't mean to scare you. Thanks for waiting for me."

"No problem." He hadn't meant to play a joke on me! Heart slowing down, I turned back toward the wall and peeked at the football field. My shoulders slumped. The girls were gone. Crap. I'd wanted to hear Mercedes's response. Sighing, I swung back to Clarik.

"I got held up by Mr. Parton," he continued. "He said he'd heard you and I were friends and asked if I knew why you'd ditched his class yesterday."

Tensing, I crossed my arms over my middle. Sunlight poured over Clarik's face, making his dark hair appear spun with gold. His eyes gleamed like twin blue sapphires. "What'd you tell him?" I asked.

"That I didn't know." He winked at me. "Which is the truth."

"Thank you." I relaxed. With everything that had gone wrong lately, I hadn't wanted to add Mr. Parton to the mix. That was a torture better suited to, well, never. "So what did you want to see me about?" I bit my lip. "Your note didn't say."

Clarik's amusement slowly faded and he regarded me intently. "I just wanted to ask if you were okay. After lunch yesterday . . ."

I forced myself to laugh and wave away his concern. "Just a bad day. I'm better now. Really." How could one boy be so cute? He was wearing jeans and a gray T-shirt, untucked. His hair was messy, a little wavy, and his eyelashes were so long they cast shadows over his cheeks.

"Can I tell you a secret?" he said, leaning toward me.

A cool breeze danced between us, wafting my hair over my face. Staring up and into his eyes, I brushed the strands aside. "Yes." I nearly cringed at how breathless I sounded.

"The real reason I asked you to meet me was so I could ask you to go to Bobby's party with me."

I gulped. Ohmygod. He was asking me out on a date. A go-somewhere-together date. "I—I don't know," I found myself saying, a wave of nervousness sweeping through me. Damn it, I'd meant to say yes.

I'd never been on a date before. What if I made a fool of myself? What if I got food stuck in my teeth or walked out of the bathroom with toilet paper on my shoe?

"Would you say yes if I asked you to meet me there?" he asked, determined.

I gulped again, but this time I nodded.

Slowly his lips inched into a smile. "Then I'll see you there."

Saturday night arrived all too soon and not soon enough. Which meant it was time to leave for Bobby's party. Which meant I would soon see Clarik.

Why had I agreed to go? I wondered nervously, staring at my reflection in the mirror. My tight, vinyl dress fit perfectly, the hem a few inches above my knees. I'd dug out my knee-high boots and they hugged the length of my calves.

"I look like a dominatrix," I muttered. No way was I going to change, however. I'd spent all of Friday evening and all of today rummaging through my closet, generally driving myself insane. Picking this outfit had nearly killed me, and I wasn't going to relive the process for something different.

My hair flowed down my back, the blue highlights the only color I wore (besides black, that is). I had tied black ribbons up my arms, and sprinkled dark glitter over my skin.

Honk. Honk. Hooonk.

Oh God. My ride was here. My palms began to sweat and my heart kicked into overdrive. I was suddenly glad I hadn't agreed to let Clarik pick me up. Already I wanted to throw up and he wasn't even in the vicinity.

"Jade," my dad called. "Taylor is waiting."

"I'm coming," I told him. My gaze roved over my reflection one last time. This was my last chance to add a necklace or touch up my makeup. Maybe I should add more gloss to my lips. Maybe I should wear my strappy heels instead of boots.

Hooooonk.

"Jade."

"Coming! Jeez." Deciding to do nothing more, I grabbed my velvet handbag and dashed out of my room. My dad was waiting by the front door, holding it open. I kissed him good-bye.

"Be careful," he said. "Mercedes isn't going to be at the party, is she?"

"Dad. Please." Without another word, I raced to Taylor Bale's red Sentra and scooted inside. Taylor was—or had been—one of Mercedes's best friends. She'd never called me a freak, not to my face at least, but she'd never spoken a word in my favor, either. The main target of *her* evil had been Robb.

"Hey, Taylor." There it was again—guilt for socializing with (and actually enjoying) my true friends' enemies. "Thanks for picking me up."

"What are you calling me Taylor for? You always call me Cheesy."

My face scrunched in confusion. "Why do I call you that?"

"Uh, hello, because I'm always smiling. You're the one who gave me the name."

O-kay. Hadn't known that.

The car sped into motion. "Daaamn, girl," Taylor—uh, Cheesy—said when we were soaring down the highway. "You look wicked hot."

"Thanks." She looked great, too. Her dark hair was twisted in ropes on top of her head and she wore a tight black bodysuit. If this were real life— *Stop, don't think like that. It's not. Your real friends don't want to hang with you.*

I hated to admit this, but the Barbies-now-Goths grew on me with every minute that passed. Like a virus. Or a fungus. With every smile they gave me, every sweet thing they did for me—like pick me up so I wouldn't have to drive—I forgot the way they used to treat me and my friends.

A week ago, I would have sworn to God that I'd never speak to any member of the Barbie clan, never hang with them. Never forgive them. Now look at me. At this rate, I was going to have to start reminding myself that I preferred individuality over popularity.

"I missed you at the Coffin Club meeting," she said. "Why'd you skip?"

Okay, I really had to ask. "What exactly is the Coffin Club?"

"Duh. Like you don't know. We get together one day a

week and talk about death, that kind of thing. This week's meeting really sucked without you. We ended up leaving early without planning our funerals or anything."

"Sorry," I said, and made a mental note not to attend next week's meeting, either. Death was Linnie's thing, not mine.

"This is going to be *the* party, isn't it?" Cheesy said. "Frightalicious. Better than Bobby's homecoming party last year. Do you remember that or were you crazy tanked like me?" She didn't give me time to answer, not that I had one. "I hear that new boy, Clarik, is going to be there, and he is so hot. Mysterious, you know. He doesn't belong to a single clique—that I know of. Maybe he thinks he's too good for all of us."

Hearing Clarik's name made me nervous again. "Maybe he likes everyone."

She shrugged, as if that wasn't even an option. "I've thought about asking him out, but I don't want to seem too easy. Be easy, yes. Seem it, no." She laughed, carefree. Unconcerned. "What would you do? Ask him out? I bet you would. You're, like, the bravest girl in the known universe."

Me? Brave? I wish. I didn't feel brave at the moment. I could actually throw up.

"So would you do it?" she continued. "Ask him out, I mean?"

"Well," I said reluctantly, "*he* kind of asked *me* out."

Her mouth flailed open. "Really? What'd you say? You said yes, didn't you? I can tell you're crushing on him, but what about Bobby? He's your boyfriend, and the two of you have been dating for, like, ever."

"Hardly." I had absolutely no interest in Bobby anymore. He was nice enough (when he wasn't telling people we were sleeping together), definitely cute enough, but the sense of must-have I'd once experienced every time I looked at him was gone.

"Ohmygod, did you two break up? You did, didn't you? Let me guess. You heard about the slut he nailed from Moore a few weeks ago. Well, good riddance. I bet he's tainted now with a thousand diseases."

No, I hadn't heard. Had Mercedes? Wait. Were he and Mercedes even dating before we entered the game or had they broken up? I'd lost track. Still. I massaged my temples, trying to ward off the oncoming ache. Mercedes wasn't my friend, but even she deserved better than a cheating boyfriend.

"So would it, like, be okay if *I* talked to Bobby?" Cheesy asked. "I won't if you don't want me to, so you can tell me the truth. I don't want to poach on your property, but he is sooo hot."

Okay. Seriously. Did the girl change love interests as often as she changed underwear? "Be my guest. He's all yours."

A grin spread across her entire face. "Very fright."

We arrived at the party fashionably late. Music blared from the house and kids tumbled from doors and windows (spilling beer and laughing) as they rolled around on the perfectly manicured lawn. I guess there'd already been some wicked crazy hookups because a few of them were making out. Asian Goth was sucking on former footballer Matt Henassey's neck. And—was that a band geek feeling up a former cheerleader on top of a cherry red Mustang?

Were Bobby's parties always like this? I'd always secretly wondered what happened when the "cool" kids got together. I'd expected gossiping and laughing, not this . . . wildness. Wanting to see everything at once, I wove my way through the crowd. Cheesy chatted continuously at my side.

"Look, Jade's here," I heard someone say.

"Hi, Jade."

"Can I get you a drink, Jade? Beer? Mixed?"

"No thanks." I didn't mind drinking but I already felt out of control, and I didn't need alcohol to make it worse. No telling what I'd blurt out. I stepped inside the house, which proved to be more cramped than the yard. The living room furniture was crammed with Goths. I don't think I'd ever seen so many black halter tops, short pleated skirts, or piercings.

There was a group of kids sitting around the coffee table, playing with a Ouija board. They were the very people who used to call me "evil" for doing the same. They motioned me to join them, but I shook my head.

The music was loud. So loud, in fact, my ears rang and a slight vibration glided down my spine. People were dancing wildly in every direction, heads shaking, hair flying. I'd never seen my classmates so undisciplined. People ran back and forth through the different rooms, playing tag. A beach ball was being slapped through the air.

Behind me, I heard a group of boys laughing about "freaks." I turned, only to see Mercedes being escorted to the door. She was soaked, her ice blue shirt and pants plastered to her body as if she'd been pushed into a pool or hosed down with beer. "You don't belong here," one of the boys slurred with a laugh.

"Yes, I do!" she growled.

"Get lost, freak."

Her tortured eyes darted around the room, then clashed with mine for a split second. The front door was slammed in her face, and the boys high-fived. Unbidden, I felt myself moving toward the door. I didn't know what I was going to do; I just knew I shouldn't let her leave without saying something.

"Come on," Cheesy said, gripping my arm and tugging me forward. "Let's circle and scope before we decide who to hang with."

Really, there was nothing I could do for Mercedes, I admitted to myself. I'd talk to her another day. "I think I'd rather find somewhere to stand." So I could watch and see *everything*.

"Okay," she said, disappointed but still moving. "Look, there's Avery. And there's Michelle. Hey Michelle!"

My gaze followed the direction in which she pointed, and I spotted Avery talking and laughing in a shadowed corner with a boy I didn't recognize. Beside them was Michelle, a redhead with more curves than a highway. She held a beer bottle and was dancing to the beat of the music.

Next, my gaze snagged on Bobby. He was whispering in a

girl's ear. The Goth underclassman beamed up at him with worship in her eyes. As he spoke, his eyes roved over the crowd. He spied me and stopped talking. He dismissed the girl without a backward glance and strode toward me. I jolted to a stop.

"Go on without me," I told Cheesy. "There's something I have to do."

"You sure?"

"Positive."

"Okay." She nodded and skipped away.

I didn't want to talk to Bobby right now. What should I do?

"Jade," a delicious voice said in my ear.

I whipped around. My heart skipped a beat and my knees gave a little shake. "Hey." I had to shout to be heard over the music.

Clarik motioned to the back door with a tilt of his chin. I bit my lip and nodded. Grinning, he clasped my hand and tugged me through the house. I gave Bobby the same treatment he'd given the girl and didn't look back.

Even though Clarik wore jeans and a white T-shirt, even though his hair wasn't dyed and he wore no face paint, no one called him a freak. Why was that? Were they afraid of him? He *did* look fierce and strong and ready to kick ass.

He led me into the backyard and my nervousness increased with every step. What were we going to talk about? What if I sounded dumb? Though it wasn't even close to Christmas, lights hung and glittered around a breathtaking white gazebo. Lush green leaves twined the crisscrossed wood.

"This is better," he said, facing me. He leaned against the wood, seeming relaxed and at ease. "We can hear each other now."

I plucked a dewy leaf from one of the slats. "So . . ." I said. I cleared my throat. *You weren't nervous that day in the parking lot,* I told myself. *Why are you nervous now?* "What have you been up to this weekend?"

He shrugged. "Cars, computers, and aggravating my uncle. The usual, I guess. What about you?"

Soooo not the usual. "Aggravating my dad, I guess."

His mouth lifted into that smile I was coming to love and his blue eyes twinkled. "I'm glad you came tonight."

"Me, too." Did I sound as lame to him as I did to myself? "Listen, I meant to apologize to you yesterday but got distracted. I truly am sorry about ditching you for lunch the other day. Did you get to eat before you went back to school?"

He nodded. "I grabbed a hamburger."

"Good." I ran my bottom lip between my teeth. "Did you get in trouble with your uncle for not bringing me back?"

"Not too much." A long pause slithered between us. Then, "I, uh, think we should try again soon."

My forehead wrinkled in confusion as I replayed our conversation in my mind and came up blank. "Try what?"

He coughed and looked away, past me, past the yard. "To eat. Together. On a date. Where I actually pick you up."

Ohmygod, ohmygod, ohmygod. "I would like that," I said. Very much. I wouldn't let nerves stop me this time.

Cheesy thought I was brave. It was time I acted that way.

Clarik's entire body relaxed (I hadn't realized he'd stiffened), and he grinned. "We'll actually eat this time, right?"

I laughed, surprised by how calm I suddenly felt. "Yes, we'll eat. I promise." My laugh slowly tapered to quiet, though, as I realized I'd have to stay in this fake reality to keep my promise. If I went back to my real reality, he might not remember that he'd asked me out. He might even think he'd asked Mercedes out, since everyone had confused our actions after the switch.

"What's wrong?" he asked me. He stepped toward me.

"Nothing," I said, unsure in that moment whether I wanted to return to the other reality—or stay in this one for a while longer. A lot longer.

"Maybe we could see a movie, too," he suggested. "What kind of movies do you like? Wait. Here's a better question. What's your favorite movie of all time?"

My cheeks burned bright with a blush. God, I hated when people asked me this. "*Romancing the Stone*," I admitted. I could have lied, but didn't think I should have to.

His eyes widened. "No way. You're kidding me, right?"

I felt my blush spread to my neck and collarbone. "No."

"I never would have pegged you for the type."

My back straightened and my shoulders squared. "What did you think my type was?"

"Not . . . romance-y. *Underworld* maybe."

What was that supposed to mean? "Well, what about you? What's your favorite movie of all time?"

"*Hackers,*" he said without hesitation. "A boy is arrested for writing a virus and—" He stopped himself. "Sorry. I know it's old but I've seen it, like, a thousand times."

"I would have pegged you for the *Terminator* type."

His lips twitched. "Then we were both wrong."

"In a good way?" I couldn't help but ask.

"In a good way," he said with a nod. "So what do you do in your free time? Besides pulling the strings of your puppets, that is."

"I do *not* have any puppets." I laughed, because I knew I lied. I still felt a little guilty about it, but I liked that more and more each day.

When my gaze again met Clarik's, my laughter died a quick death. His gaze had become intense. I swallowed the sudden lump in my throat. "What are you thinking about?" My voice was breathless.

"You're pretty when you smile." He stepped closer to me. "I'm thinking about kissing you."

I blinked. Ohmygod, ohmygod, ohmygod. My mouth went dry, but I raised my chin. Yes! This was it! I wasn't afraid. I wanted to kiss him. So badly. My first kiss.

Slowly, he inched his face down. His breath fanned my cheek. My eyelids began to close. Any second his mouth would brush mine. His tongue would—

The back door slid open. Avery and Cheesy tumbled out, giggling. Clarik and I froze in place, startled, then jumped apart. "Jade, you naughty thing," Avery said. She and Cheesy stumbled over to me. "We've been looking everywhere for you. Tommy Barrett is doing a striptease on the kitchen table. You have to see."

"I nearly died laughing." Cheesy giggled. "I think Bobby is going to dance, too."

"I think I'll stay out here," I told them, flicking Clarik a glance. He'd backed away from me and had his hands stuffed in his pockets.

Avery's mouth dipped into a pout. Cheesy lost her grin (for once). "But . . ."

"It's okay," Clarik said. He backed off another step. "I've got to go anyway."

Now *I* found myself frowning. "But . . ." I said in a perfect mimic of Cheesy. I'd come here to see him and I wasn't ready for him to leave.

"See you around, Jade." Without another word, he strode away.

Puzzled, I watched him. Why had he taken off so fast? What had changed his easy mood? I wasn't given time to think about the oddity of it. Avery grabbed my hand and tugged me inside the house.

"What kind of friend would I be if I let you miss all the fun?" she said. "Come on."

I could have protested, but didn't. *Fun.* How long had it been since I'd had any? Surely an eternity had passed. The prospect was tempting. Heady.

Inside the house, someone thrust a beer at me and I

grabbed it to keep it from falling to the floor. Avery and Cheesy laughingly toasted me. I sipped, but they both shook their head.

"Uh, uh, uh," Avery said. "Drink. You've got to loosen up if you want to have fun!"

Fun, I mused again. I gulped back half the bottle. Normally I didn't like the taste of beer, but found myself finishing the rest as we approached the kitchen table. I even drained another.

Amid cheers and whistles, several boys were, indeed, dancing on the table surface. "Take it off," a girl shouted with glee.

Bobby swung his hips and reached behind his head. He tugged off his shirt, revealing a strong, tanned stomach. Girls screamed with encouragement. His eyes met mine; he tossed the shirt at me. The material draped my head and a wave of dizziness hit me.

Laughing, I fought my way free. At that moment, I felt carefree, like I could do anything. Like nothing mattered. Not Clarik's disappearance, not the virtual reality game. Not my friends. I spun the shirt over my head and tossed it back at Bobby.

He jumped down, girls moaning in disappointment. He approached me, saying, "Let's dance."

I let him usher me into the living room, where kids still bumped and grinded. I only stumbled twice. He wrapped his arms around me and pulled me close. My cheek meshed into his bare shoulder.

"You look smokin' tonight," he said.

"Thanks." The word was slurred, even to my own ears. I frowned.

"I'm glad you came. We haven't gotten to spend enough time together lately."

At one time, I would have given both my kidneys (maybe even my liver) to be in this exact spot: Bobby's arms. Now it just felt . . . wrong.

"Do you want to stay the night?" he asked huskily.

My frown deepened. "No. My dad expects me home." My dizzy gaze slid over the room, looking for an escape. Home sounded good just then. My eyes landed on the far window. I saw a blur of blond hair and . . . was that Mercedes? I stiffened. Yes, that's exactly who it was. She was crouched at the window, peering into the room. At *me*. Her eyes were dark with anger, yet her mouth was soft with sadness and her cheeks were streaked with tears.

A dark slash appeared beside her, claiming her attention. My chin tilted to the side, and I—my mouth fell open. Clarik. Clarik was with her, was speaking to her. He wiped away one of her tears. What were they doing out there? Together? They'd kissed once. What if they did again?

I jerked from Bobby and leapt into motion.

"Hey," he called. "Where are you going?"

I pushed through the crowd, around furniture, fighting the dizziness in my head as I stormed outside. But by the time I got out there, they were gone.

My head pounded, my eyes burned. I moaned. My mouth felt as dry as cotton, and my stomach . . . dear Lord, my stomach. It churned and twisted and cramped.

"Coffee," I heard a girl mutter. "I need coffee."

I recognized Avery's voice. Confused, I forced myself to sit up. Rubbing my temples, I searched my surroundings. I was in my room, I realized, on my bed. Avery was beside me, and two other bodies were strewn out on my floor.

"What are you doing here?" I asked her.

"We drove you home, remember, and decided to crash here."

"Rather than crash on the road," Cheesy said, cringing. She sat up and closed her eyes. "Shit, my head. Where's the Tylenol?"

"I feel fine," Michelle said. She stretched her arms over her head and bounded up with a grin.

"Why aren't you in pain?" I demanded.

She grinned. "Unlike you guys, I stopped after one beer."

"Bitch," Avery muttered.

Michelle chuckled, the sound deep and hardy. "You're just jealous."

How weird, I thought, to wake up with the Barbies in my room. Even weirder, they were here willingly and I didn't want to kick them out.

We took turns in the bathroom, and all three of them borrowed clothes from me. When we were dressed—which translated to hair pulled back in a ponytail, no makeup, and jeans and T-shirts—we piled into Michelle's car. My dad was at work, so I didn't have to worry about getting his permission.

At Avery's insistence, Michelle drove us to Starbucks. We were soon seated at a table, sucking back Caramel Macchiatos.

"Last night was fun," Cheesy said.

"Too fun," Avery replied, rubbing her temples.

"My head is still pounding." Several wisps of hair fell at my temples, and I tucked the strands behind my ear. "Remind me never to drink again."

"So what's the deal with you and Clarik?" Avery asked. "You two looked freakishly cozy in my backyard."

"He asked her out," Cheesy answered for me. She sipped her coffee.

Talking about Clarik reminded me of the party. Had I really seen him lurking at the window, with Mercedes of all people, or had that been a drunken dream? Deep down, I doubted it had been a dream. A girl could hope, though. I didn't know what I'd do if I found out they were friends—with benefits?

Eyes narrowing on me, Michelle swirled a spoon in her half-empty cup. "Clarik asked you out and this is the first we hear about it?"

"What about Bobby?" Avery's tone was devoid of emotion, giving no hint to her thoughts.

My head hurt too much to try and soften my words. "I'm not interested in your brother, Avery. I'm sorry." I sipped at my drink, feeling a little stronger as the hot, sweet liquid slid into my stomach.

The corners of her lips turned down. "What about our plan? You were going to marry him, and we were going to be sisters."

"Plans change," I said, not knowing what else I *could* say.

Silence.

Then she sighed. "You guys would have ended up getting a divorce, anyway. You're on and off more times than that slut Wendy Benedict's panties."

"Jade said it was okay if I made a play for Bobby," Cheesy said.

Avery barely flicked her a glance. "So," she said to me. I could tell she was upset I wouldn't be dating her brother, more upset that Cheesy wanted him, but she was trying not to show it. "What did you tell Clarik?"

"I said yes," I answered truthfully. I stared down at my cup, watching the caramel melt through the dark liquid. "I'm nervous about it," I admitted then. It was so natural, talking with them.

"Why?" Michelle drained the rest of her coffee. "You've been on thousands of dates."

I wish. "What do you do when you're out on a date? What do you talk about?"

Avery shrugged. "We talk about, well, me."

"Why don't you cast a spell or something?" Michelle lifted her knee and anchored it between her and the table. "You could cast a love spell. Or maybe a memory spell if you do something stupid."

"Spells aren't my thing," I said. "I don't know how to cast them."

"Oh. Hmmm. Well, you could get him drunk, then he'll have a good time no matter what you do or say."

"She could kiss him," Cheesy suggested. "That's what I do when there's an uncomfortable silence."

"That's because you're a lip slut," Avery retorted.

Cheesy gasped. "I am not."

"I bet you've kissed every boy at our school, Easy Cheesy, if not more. More than kissing and more than the boys at our school, that is."

"That is so false. So false."

As they argued back and forth, I grinned. They cared for one another, I could tell. Just like Avery and Bobby, a brother and sister. These girls weren't related, but they still cared. There was genuine affection in their eyes and their insults were teasing rather than biting. That was the same relationship I'd had with Erica and Linnie. I missed that.

Was that part of my life over forever?

I sighed, not wanting to think about that now. At least I had this group of friends. A group of friends it was becoming harder and harder to think of as fakes. "Come on, girls. Enough fighting. Let's go to the bookstore and forget all our troubles, if only for a little while."

chapter eleven

*When someone dies, they leave pieces of
themselves behind. I get that. I just wish
they left better pieces.*

Monday ended up being a real suckfest.

Ms. Hamilton failed to show up. Mercedes ditched and, surprisingly enough, I missed her. She was the only one who truly understood what I was going through. Linnie, Erica, and Robb glared at me every time they saw me (at least they'd stopped flipping me off), and half the girls in the school were wearing the exact outfit I'd worn to Bobby's party.

Sighing, I strode into Parton's class with my nerves already on edge. I'd spend the entire hour, if needed, thinking of ways to hunt Ms. Hamilton down. Clarik, I noticed, sat at the back of the room. My heart gave a little flutter, just like it had at the party.

He motioned me over with a crook of his finger. His expression was blank and gave nothing away. What thoughts tumbled through his mind? If he planned to cut me loose so he could pursue Mercedes. . . . My hands balled into fists.

The chairs around him were already occupied, but he said something to one of the boys, who glanced at me, nodded, and hurriedly unfolded to his feet and moved to another chair.

"Thank you," I said, slipping into the now vacant desk.

Clarik leaned toward me, opening his mouth to say something. Before he could speak, I said, "Were you with Mercedes Saturday night or was that my imagination? I thought I saw you guys at the window."

Something I didn't recognize fluttered over his expression. "I found her outside. She was crying, so I took her home. There was nothing more to it than that."

Sweet, sweet relief enveloped me. "You took off so suddenly, I—"

"Decided to dance with a half-dressed Bobby Richards," he finished for me. Finally, his face took on an emotion I recognized. Anger. His blue eyes flashed with it; his mouth pulled taut with it.

"Nothing happened, I swear." Was he, dare I hope, jealous?

"I didn't like it," he growled quietly.

He was. Clarik was jealous. "I don't plan on doing it again," I growled back, just as quietly. I was trying not to smile. No boy had ever been jealous over me before.

"Good."

"Good."

Slowly his features relaxed and he studied my face for a long while. "So what's this I hear about you and Mercedes getting arrested?" he asked, changing the subject.

Color bloomed in my cheeks, scalding hot. "We, uh, did a little breaking and entering. That's all."

"That's all, huh?" He tsked under his tongue.

I was saved from a response as the bell rang.

"Good morning, class," Mr. Parton said as he strode inside the room. "Let's get settled so we can begin."

I bent down and gathered my pencils, book, and paper. Clarik ignored him and continued speaking to me. "I've been arrested twice, and would never have pegged you as the type to risk it."

Frowning, I organized my desktop. I didn't know whether to take offense to his words or be happy with them—obviously, I was leaning toward offense. That was the second time he'd accused me of being a "type." "What type do you think I am?" Wait. I shook my head. "And why did you get arrested?"

"You're too sweet. I should have guessed you had a hidden wild streak, though, when you told me your favorite movie." He leaned a little closer to me, so close his breath fanned my ear. "And I'll never tell."

All right. I was happy with his words. Totally. No offense to be taken when he thought I was sweet and had a wild streak. My frown disappeared. Boys just didn't say stuff like that to me. "Boring," surprisingly, yes. "Freakish," absolutely. "Now you've made your crimes a puzzle to be solved."

He blinked in surprise—and hope. "Knowing I've been in jail doesn't scare you?"

"No." Linnie had once been arrested for shoplifting, but she wasn't a bad person. Robb, too, had been taken downtown for public intoxication. People did stupid things. That didn't make them bad. "Drinking and driving? Painting the side of a building?"

"Excuse me, Miss Leigh."

Groaning inwardly, I turned in my chair and faced Mr. Parton. My mouth fell open. He was staring at me, his eyes heavily lined with black, his lips rimmed with black. He wore all black and his (thinning) hair was in spikes. I hadn't seen him since entering the game. "Yeah?" I managed.

There was a thick, heavy, palm-sweating pause.

His features gradually softened. "I'm glad you made it today. You missed Friday. Were you ill? I didn't get a note, but that's okay. I was just worried about you."

"What?" I shook my head. Surely I had misheard. Mr. Parton wouldn't let his dying mother miss his class without a notarized doctor's note. He was *that* controlling.

"Poor thing." He walked to me and patted my arm, as sweet as the Caramel Macchiato I'd had from Starbucks. "If you start to feel sick, just get up and go. You don't have to wait for permission."

"I—thanks?"

"Anytime. We can't have our best student suffering, now can we?" He turned around and strode to the front of the class.

Best student? Open-mouthed, I watched his retreating back. His behavior should not have astounded me, I guess, and maybe I should have expected it. But it did and I hadn't. Not from him. I slunk in my chair and, yes, I smiled with satisfaction.

"Hey," Clarik whispered, reclaiming my attention. "I noticed you in the office several times today, asking for Ms. Hamilton."

"Yes. Have you seen her?"

"No." His head canted to the side. "Are you and Mercedes in some kind of trouble? She's desperate to find Ms. Hamilton, too."

There was an odd inflection in his voice. Did he know something? Silent, I studied his earnest expression. No, surely not. No way he *could* know—unless Mercedes had told him. "What did Mercedes tell you?" I didn't want him to know, to think I was crazy.

"She just mentioned she needed to find Ms. Hamilton, and she had the same wild gleam in her eyes that you've got now."

"We need to talk to her . . . about a special project we're working on," I finally answered. Truth.

He pursed his lips. "Maybe I can help."

My forehead crinkled as I gazed over at him. "How?"

"She's sick, right, and won't be back at school for a while."

"I highly doubt she's sick," I said, my tone dry.

"Well, if we find her home address, we find her."

"She's not listed."

"Not in the phone book, no, but if she's like my mom, she brings her mail to work so she can read it and avoid doing actual work. Her address will be on the envelopes."

Oh. My. God. I straightened in my chair with a jolt. He was right. *Dummy,* my mind chastised. *Why didn't you think of that?* Maybe I hadn't wanted to think of it. Maybe I'd been having too much fun here. Annnnd, there was the guilt. "I need to get into her office."

His lips twitched and his eyes glowed with triumph, and in that moment he'd never looked hotter. "More breaking and entering, huh?"

My fingers clenched and unclenched, I was so eager to begin. "Will you help me?"

He smiled, just a little naughty and waaay sexy. "Absolutely."

"Hey, Cher. Can I talk to you for a minute? In private?"

Even though he wasn't talking to me, the tone of Clarik's deep, sexy voice melted me from inside out. Cher must have felt the same, because she patted her red curls, rose, and approached the counter where Clarik stood. I watched from the corner of the hallway, ducking every time her all-seeing eyes wandered in my direction.

My palms were sweaty and my ribs ached from the megawatt force of my heartbeat. I didn't care if I got caught. I mean, please. Haven't you heard? Sweet little Jade can do no wrong. No, I feared failure. Again. I feared finding nothing. And—

I hated to admit this, but part of me feared finding *something*.

"What do you need, Clarik?" Cher propped her elbows on the countertop that separated them and rested her chin in her upraised palms.

"I need an off-campus pass."

"Tsk, tsk, tsk. You know I can't give you one without permission from your parents."

"But I don't live with my parents," he said sadly.

I rolled my eyes. Laying it a little thick, Clarik.

"Oh, that's right." Cher patted his hand. "I forgot. I'm sorry."

The other secretary, Gail, joined them. "What's going on?"

"Clarik wants an off-campus pass," Cher informed her.

"But I don't have parents to give me permission," he added in that same, sad tone.

I gave another eye roll. An Academy Award winner he was not. He practically radiated the term "bullshit."

"What about your guardian?" Gail asked with a knowing gleam in her eyes.

Still, his acting did the job. With both women distracted, I crouched and sulked from the corner, crawling on my hands and knees to the office. Hammy's door was closed and I prayed to God it wasn't—locked. Crap! It *was* locked. The knob refused to turn, even a little.

Twisting, staying low, I circled my gaze around the office. Who would have a spare key? Cher, most likely. She'd have to be able to get inside, just in case she needed something. The vice principal, too, would need to be able to enter.

So where did they keep their spares and how could I steal one?

My eyes locked desperately on Clarik. "—need my inhaler," he was saying with a fake wheeze and cough. God help me. "I forgot it." His gaze met mine for a split second.

Keys, I mouthed. *Lock.* I motioned to the knob with a single jerk of my chin.

He gave an almost imperceptible nod.

"You sound like you're faking," Cher said, calling his bluff. "I bet you don't even use an inhaler. Perhaps I should call your uncle and ask. Or maybe send someone to the security booth to talk with him personally."

Clarik remained calm. "He doesn't like to be disturbed while he's at work."

"I'm sure he doesn't," she said dryly.

"Okay, look." He straightened to his full height. "The real reason I'm here is that . . ." He stared down at his tennis shoes, suddenly sheepish. "I wanted to ask you out, but I didn't know how else to approach you so I pretended to need a pass."

What?

"What?" Cher squeaked.

"What?" Gail shouted.

"I think you're hot." He leveled Cher with a bone-tingling grin.

"Uh, Clarik, you're . . . you're . . ." She struggled to form a proper response.

His eyes rounded. "Ugly? Not your type? Don't tell me I'm too young. Age doesn't matter."

He sounded so sincere *I* nearly believed he wanted to go out with the woman.

Cher scooted around the counter and placed her hands on Clarik's shoulders, telling him all the reasons she couldn't date him. He threw his arms around her for a hug, and she *hmp*ed. What the hell was he doing?

"Just give me a chance," he said, pulling slightly away from her. Without turning, he slid his arm to his side and tossed me a set of keys.

Startled, I barely caught them. I gaped down at the silver chain for half a second. Clarik, pickpocket extraordinaire. Who would have guessed? And how had he known Cher had them on her?

Their voices faded from my ears as I stretched up my arm and inserted key after key until I finally found the right one. Yes! Success. I cracked open the door and quietly crawled through the opening. Then, with barely a snap, I shut myself inside. A huge sigh of relief slipped from me.

A startled gasp rang out and an armful of papers scattered to the floor. A blond head peeked around the corner of the desk. "Jade?"

"Mercedes?"

She remained in place, eyes slitting on me. "What are you doing in here?"

"The same thing you're doing. Looking for Ms. Hamilton." I glanced back at the door. "How did you get in here? The office Nazis would never have let you in."

"You're right." The corners of her mouth curled in a slight smirk. "Linnie and Erica helped me. They bought a knockoff key from that kid, what's his name, who got busted for breaking into the school last year. Who would have thought hanging out with the freaks would have such perks?"

Jealousy sliced through me. They were *my* friends. They should have helped *me*. And where did she get off, calling them names when she'd spent time with them, talking and laughing at cheerleading practice?

Before I could respond, Mercedes crawled from behind the desk and said, "Well, don't just sit there. Do something. We don't have a lot of time." She held her Sidekick and snapped several pictures of the papers and e-mailed them to herself.

My mouth fell open as I was given a full view of her appearance. "Are you wearing black leather?"

Her cheeks reddened, the color spreading over her exposed collarbone. "Yeah. So?" She lifted her chin defiantly.

She wore thick, black eyeliner, not the subdued brown she

usually wore. Black lip liner instead of pink and a black leather catsuit. "Why are you dressed like that?"

"My mom forced me, okay? And it's the reason I didn't go to class today. Like I really want to be seen looking like the Feline Grim Reaper."

"What did Erica and Linnie say?"

"They didn't like it. Now help me go through these papers." She shoved a stack at me.

I took them blindly, saying with a suppressed smile, "You don't look so bad. You're actually kind of cute."

"Just shut up," she said, but there was no heat in her tone this time. "Do you want to get caught in here? Start looking for stuff about the game."

"Hammy's address wouldn't hurt, either."

"Yeah. If nothing else we can egg her home."

I thumbed through the papers. They were incident reports, information on specific students, and several sheets with the same gibberish I'd seen on the warehouse papers. Those I stuffed in my pockets and told Mercedes to do the same.

"I don't need to steal them and alert everyone to the fact that someone was in here. I'll print off the pictures when I get home."

Maybe I shouldn't have thrown out that Sidekick.

"What do you think they are?" she asked.

"I don't know. That's why we need to study them." I paused, trying to make myself appear nonchalant. "I hear Clarik drove you home Saturday night."

"Yeah. So?"

I grit my teeth. "So he says nothing happened."

"He's right." Pause. Changed the subject. "So how'd *you* get in the office?"

"Clarik."

She flicked me a quick glance. "So are you guys, like, dating or something?"

I popped my jaw, ran my tongue over my teeth, not really wanting to answer her, but not knowing how to respond, either.

"What if he doesn't like you when we get home?" she asked, voicing one of my deepest fears. A fear I hadn't allowed myself to dwell on. "What then?"

Maybe I paled. Maybe I radiated trepidation. Either way, she shook her head and said confidently, "You like him or the possibility wouldn't bother you so much."

"So what if I do?" My gaze slitted so much the top and bottom of my lashes intertwined. Mercedes became nothing more than a black blur. "Are you going to make another play for him?"

"What are you talking about? I've never made a play for him."

"Yeah." I snorted. "Sure."

"I didn't," she insisted.

"You kissed him in the library and fought your friends over him." Just then my gaze snagged on a set of papers with Clarik's name on them. Excited, I folded them and added them to my stash. "That's why you were punished. That's why *you needed to be taught a lesson*," I added in my best Hammy impersonation.

"I didn't kiss Clarik in the library," she said after a long pause. "And I didn't fight over him. I kissed Bobby."

"No. Way," I gasped out.

"I slapped Cheesy for telling me Bobby slept with a girl from Moore. She slapped me back and before I knew it we were rolling on the ground."

"So you didn't kiss Clarik?"

"No."

Shock—yes. Joy—definitely. Clarik hadn't . . . they had never . . . His tongue hadn't been inside her mouth! He'd never been interested in her. Only a sense of self-preservation kept me from jumping up and down, clapping and whooping like an idiot.

While I internally celebrated, Mercedes stared down at her hands, a visible change of emotion overtaking her. From haughty to unsure, in the blink of an eye. "Did you really not know about our parents?"

"No." And I wished I didn't know now. Ignorance truly was bliss. "How did you know about them?"

A long sigh seeped from her, sad and angry at the same time. "I caught them together. Kissing." She pretended to gag. "They didn't realize I'd seen them and I only recently started dropping hints that I knew."

"I'm sorry." I think, deep down, I meant the words as an apology for everything. Not just our parents, but our war with each other. Now I understood why she had reacted the way she had these past couple years.

"Yeah," she said softly. "Me, too. I think I hated you so much because of your dad. He loves you, you know. Mine won't even return my phone calls anymore."

"You have a mom who loves you," I reminded her.

"Yeah," she repeated, but she didn't sound convinced.

We searched in silence for a long while after that, the only noise the ticking of the wall clock. Maybe we were afraid to break the fragile peace we'd just established, I don't know.

Finally, I sighed. "I'm not finding anything."

"Me, either." Frowning, she threw up her hands. "What a nightmare."

"We can't stay much longer or we'll get caught, and there's no way we can explain breaking into Hammy's office."

She tangled a hand in her hair. "What should we do? I've already tried her computer, but it's password protected."

"We have *got* to find this woman."

A light tap resonated from the door; Mercedes and I stilled. Our gaze locked on each other, instantly panicked. Both of us dove under the desk as the tinkle of the handle rang in our ears. Hinges squeaked. My breath emerged choppy, blending with Mercedes's.

"Where's my key?" Cher said. "I know I locked this door."

"So . . . are you happily married or not?" Clarik. Surprisingly calm.

The shuffle of footsteps. A sigh. A pause.

"Yes. Now, I told you to go to class. I have work to do, and I can't do it with you hovering over my shoulder."

More footsteps.

"Show me the pictures of your husband again." Clarik no longer sounded quite so calm.

"Go. To. Class." Another pause. "How did these papers get on the floor?" Cher bent down. I caught sight of her hosed calf, her emerald dress hem, her knees, then her red curls as she gathered the papers around her.

Beside me, Mercedes stiffened. If Cher turned just a little to the left, she'd spot us.

"Let me help you with those," Clarik said in a rush. He raced to her side, his eyes meeting mine for a split second, then Mercedes's. His mouth snapped open, and I noticed he was pale and beaded with sweat. He used his back to block us from view. "I love to help. Yep, love it."

Cher popped to her feet. "Boy, you can*not* stay here. You have to go to class."

"Will you walk me there?"

She uttered a frustrated growl. Outside, the bell rang and the trundle of footsteps abounded.

"Please," he said.

"Fine. Let's go."

More footsteps. The door slammed shut. I peeked from behind the desk and relief poured through me. Thank God. "We're clear."

"I'm so out of here," Mercedes said, crawling out.

I followed behind her, quickly exiting the office and scrambling into the hall. At the fork, we branched in opposite directions. Unfortunately, I bumped into several students.

"Hey, watch it." Then, "Oops sorry, Jade."

"My bad, Jade," someone else said.

Finally I rounded the corner without being spotted by either of the secretaries. I jolted up and plastered myself against one of the lockers, sucking in breath after breath. That was too close!

A few minutes later, as the hallway started to empty, Cher strode around the far corner. She frowned when she spotted me. "You need to get to class, Jade."

"Yes, ma'am. I'm headed there now."

She disappeared into the office, but I remained in place. Soon Clarik, too, strode toward me. He grinned, an excited gleam in his eyes. He had to be a danger junkie. "Man, I thought we were busted."

What if he doesn't like you when we get home? Mercedes's words echoed through my mind, suddenly and without prompting. I brushed my hair out of my face, mentally brushing the sense of foreboding aside with it. "Me, too."

His grin widened. "Did you get what you needed?"

I thought about the unreadable papers I'd stolen and the folder I'd stuffed up my shirt that was filled with information about him. Still, none of it was what I'd needed to get home. "No." I sighed.

"I'm sorry." Running his lower lip between his teeth, he rested one of his arms over my head. Our noses almost touched. Several seconds ticked by and I watched a play of emotions flash over his face. Regret—which I didn't understand. Guilt—for my failure to find Hammy's address? Determination—another emotion I didn't get. "Can you come to my house after school? I can try to hack into the school's database or something and get her address that way."

I brightened, more at the thought of going to his house. "Really?"

"I'll tell you a secret," he whispered. "That's one of the reasons I was arrested. Hacking. I'm very good."

My heart skipped a beat at the thought of spending more time with him and I felt myself smiling. I wouldn't worry that his feelings for me would change when I left the game. I wouldn't worry about making a fool of myself around him. Not now. Not today.

Today I'd just enjoy being a girl who liked a boy.

"I'd like that," I said. "A lot."

He watched me silently for a bit, the soon-to-be tardy students rushing to their next class fading from our view. "You have a very pretty smile. I've told you that, right?"

"Hey, Jade," someone called before I could respond. Well, that's if internal combustion didn't count as a response.

I glanced to my left. Avery and Cheesy were skipping toward me, wide grins spreading across their faces. Erica and Linnie were behind them, glaring at me.

"A group of us are going to the mall after school," Avery said. She stopped in front of me. "Want to come?"

My gaze remained locked on Erica and I opened my mouth to refuse. Avery beat me to it. "Please say yes. We won't have any fun without you. Clarik can come, too. Besides, we need to buy you another Sidekick so I can get a hold of you twenty-four/seven. If your dad won't buy you one, I will. I have my mom's cards!"

"I'm sorry," I said at the same time Clarik said, "Yeah, I'd like that. Thanks."

Avery uttered a squeal of delight. Erica and Linnie disappeared down the hall. A part of me wanted to chase after them. A part of me didn't.

"Fright," Avery said. "We are soooo going to have a blast." She and Cheesy flounced away as quickly as they'd approached.

Clarik linked his fingers with mine and squeezed my hand, drawing my attention. "It'll be fun. I haven't hung out with a group of friends in, well. . . . We can spend a few hours with them before heading to my house."

His palm was warm against mine, calloused where mine was soft. I shivered. "Count me in."

chapter twelve

Once I cut my finger (never cut your steak while distracted). It hurt. A lot. But when the pain went away, I realized something. My finger had never felt better. Do you think it takes true pain to experience true pleasure?

Shopping with the Barbies had once been my idea of punishment. But shopping with them now, I found, was actually quite fun. Somehow they made me feel as if I were something special. A heady feeling, considering that my former friends made me feel like a giant, oozing zit every time they looked at me.

"They're out of black nail polish," Avery said with a pout.

"Buy ice blue then," I suggested. "Blue nails are fright."

"Really? Okay." Grinning, she dropped several shades of blue polish in her basket. "Do you think I should get the scarf with skeletons or daggers?"

"Why not both? You've got your mom's cards, right?"

Her grin widened. "Excellent idea!"

"You always know exactly what looks good," Cheesy said, "and that's why you have to tell me if this necklace is right for me or not." She pointed to a silver chain with black beads that dangled in the center, twisting together and forming a heart. "Will it look freakishly stupid on me?"

"No, but you'd look better in the crystal choker."

Her eyes widened on the choker in question and she reached out, palming it. "Black star for you! You're right, as always. Thank you, thank you! I'm so glad you came today. I would have been lost without you. Just imagine if I'd bought the heart necklace instead of this."

"I think they'd stop breathing if you told them it was unfright," Clarik muttered in my ear.

I chuckled, but he wasn't too far off the mark. There was a sense of power in that. Freak no longer. Now leader. My opinions were valued. My sense of style unquestioned. *But you're becoming one of the crowd* . . . I forced that thought out of my mind and concentrated on Clarik. The other boys had continuously wandered off, but Clarik had stayed by my side the entire time without protest, as if he really, *really* liked being there.

"I'm crazy hungry," Avery said after she paid for the polish and scarf. "Want to grab something to eat?"

She directed the question at me, and everyone in our little group turned to watch me expectantly. "Definitely."

"Me, too," said Cheesy.

"I'm starved, about to gnaw off my arm," said Michelle.

We headed toward the food court and had almost reached it when Bobby and his friends rejoined us. With a glare in Clarik's direction, Bobby stomped to my side and wound his arm around my waist.

"I'll buy yours, Jade," he said. "Whatever you want. Burger. Taco. Cookie. It's on me."

"Bobby said 'on me,'" one of the other boys snickered. "But he really wants to get her off." The boys hooted and whistled; the girls rolled their eyes and groaned.

I frowned and tried to gently extract myself from Bobby's hold. "I can pay for my own." I didn't mind a guy paying for my food—not that it had ever happened—I just didn't want Clarik to think Bobby meant something more to me than he actually did.

"I'll pay for Jade's," Clarik said. He grabbed my hand and tugged me to his side.

Hey, wait a second . . .

Bobby's scowl became darker as he grabbed for me. One boy had one arm, the other had the other arm, and they took turns pulling me back and forth. I was the rope in an angry tug-of-war. Were they going to fight over me? Avery and the others seemed to think so. They raced to the wall, plastering themselves against it.

"I've seen your car. You can't afford shit. Besides that, you're not her boyfriend," said Bobby.

"Neither are you," said Clarik.

"She and I have history, man. A lot of it."

"No, we don't," I said.

Clarik's gaze narrowed on me. "You told me you two weren't dating."

I jerked away from both of them. There was no way I could explain this. No way he would believe me.

"Something's up with this guy, Jade," Bobby said. "He's been scheming on you since his first day, watching you, following you. I don't like it."

Avery grabbed me and tugged me to her side. I kept my eyes on the boys. Bobby's scowl was now lethal and he shoved Clarik in the shoulders. Clarik growled and returned the shove.

"Touch me again," Clarik bit out, "and I'll kick your ass. Understand?"

"Think you're big enough to take me on? Try it then. I dare you."

Clarik grinned, an anticipatory gleam in his eyes. "Believe me, it will be my pleasure."

Before they decided to kill each other, I moved from the wall and jumped between them. "Stop. Okay. Just stop."

Bobby held out his arm to block me from their circle.

"I'm not stopping till he leaves. He's not one of us, Jade, and you need to realize that. He belongs with the freaks. Look at him. He's not wearing any eyeliner, and his hair has no real color."

I saw Clarik stiffen, saw his muscles clench as they prepared to spring forward. "He's not a freak," I snapped. "Just because someone's different, or new, or you don't understand them, doesn't mean they're bad."

"I didn't ask for your opinion," Bobby spewed out.

"Go back to the wall, Jade," Clarik said flatly. His eyes had gone cold.

Both boys were beyond common sense. Exasperated, I threw up my hands. "Fine. Kill each other, but don't expect me to watch. I'm out of here. Come on, girls."

I walked away without a backward glance.

"Don't leave, Jade," Avery called shakily. "I have to stay with my brother."

Okay, so the girls hadn't followed me. So much for me being their leader. I didn't look back, didn't slow. I'd walk home and they could find someone else to advise them on their nail polish and jewelry choices.

"That's right. Run. You coward," I heard Bobby shout. I bit the inside of my cheek, debating whether to turn around and slap him or just keep moving, getting as far away from him as possible. How dare he talk to me like that, that rotten piece of—

"Hey," Clarik said, suddenly beside me and keeping pace.

I jerked in surprise. "You're not staying to fight?"

"I'd rather be with you." He curled his fingers around my arm and tugged me to a gentle stop. "I'm sorry I let Bobby get to me. He yelled at you, and well . . ." His voice trailed off. "I reacted. Don't be mad."

I didn't look at him. I looked past him, past the stores bursting with Goths (we really had taken over the world), past the aisles of black shoes and black clothes. I sighed. "When you put it like that, I can't really stay mad, now can I?"

He grinned slowly. "I like you, Jade Leigh. I really do."

What if he doesn't like you when we get home? Well, hell. Why wouldn't that question stay out of my head? My hands clenched. I'd told myself I wouldn't worry about that today. Still, I found myself saying, "Why do you like me, Clarik?"

A blank mask shuttered over his features. "Just . . . because."

"Because why?" I insisted.

Twin pink circles stained his cheeks. "Are you really going to make me say it?"

"Yes," I said, but my stomach twisted painfully.

Looking uncomfortable, he massaged the back of his neck with his free hand. "You're pretty, okay? You're funny and smart and I like how I feel when I'm around you." His other hand lowered to mine and he linked our fingers. "Do you like me?" he asked hesitantly.

My cheeks flushed, an exact copy of his. I'd made him say it, so I could do no less. "Yes," I said quietly.

"Why?"

I stared down at our hands. His were bigger than mine, the bones thicker, stronger. His skin was several shades darker and he had a long scar that slashed from the nail bed of his index finger to the top of his wrist.

"You're cute," I said. Inhaling deeply, I took in the scent of hamburgers, cookies, and multiple layers of clashing perfumes. Underneath it all was his scent. Clarik's. Soap and leather with a hint of motor oil. "I like your smile. And I like how I feel when you look at me."

He didn't respond for several, gut-wrenching seconds. Then, "I'm glad we got that settled." He slung his arm over my shoulder. "So what do we do? Now that I like you and you like me."

"Now," I said, clearing my throat, "we go to your house and see what we can dig up on Principal Hammy."

"All right."

"We'll have to—" My gaze widened as I caught a glimpse of a familiar blond head. There, in the food court, was Mercedes. She wasn't alone, either. Erica, Linnie, and Robb surrounded her.

Their table was in back, and the four of them were in the middle of an animated, laughing conversation. Mercedes had removed all traces of the Goth feline look and now wore a pink tank top with white pants. She wasn't even glancing around, making sure no one saw her with the "freaks." It looked like she was instructing them on how to use their new Sidekicks.

I thought they'd told her no, that the phones would make them conformists.

I experienced a very familiar pang of jealousy. At least Robb had stopped thinking of himself as Mercedes's boyfriend. He and Linnie were making goo-goo eyes at each other—please tell me I don't do that with Clarik.

Funnily enough, I wasn't upset by their love match this time. Better he be with Linnie than with the fake Mercedes.

"Okay, what's put you in this trance?" Clarik asked. His gaze followed the direction of mine. He shook his head. "Ah, your special project partner and number one enemy."

"Yes," I said out of habit.

He rubbed his palm up and down my upper arm. "What made you two hate each other so much?"

"Our parents are . . . dating." I almost gagged on the last word.

"Ah. No need to say any more. My mom once dated my football coach. I woke up one morning to find the man eating cereal at my kitchen table." He shuddered.

"Did you jump him?"

"Something like that," he muttered.

As I watched, Avery and Bobby strode toward their table. My eyebrows drew together. "What are they going to do?"

A second passed in silence and Clarik frowned. "Nothing good, I can tell you that much. I hate bullies."

He radiated vehemence, and there was a raw, vulnerable quality to him now. I didn't have time to question him.

Bobby slid into the seat next to Mercedes, knocking her off. She hit the ground with a thump, but quickly jolted to her feet. She even slapped him on the back of the head.

"Dumb-ass," I heard her shout. "When I get back to the real world, I'm going to make you pay for that."

"Don't hit me," he said with quiet menace. "And the hell you will, you crazy bitch."

"Don't ever push me down again. Now move!"

He crossed his arms over his thick linebacker chest. "Make me."

"Leave her alone," Robb snapped.

Bobby squared off with him, determined, I guess, to get his fight from someone. He'd probably been a little afraid of Clarik's lack of fear, so turned his sights on Robb, who had no muscle to protect himself. "Come over here and make me, Stilts."

Robb's face reddened and a shudder of fear rocked him, but he remained in place, ready to fight if he had to. "I will."

"Come on, then," Bobby said, propping up his legs with complete nonchalance. "I'm waiting."

"Stop." Mercedes slapped the tabletop. Her pale hair bobbed over her shoulders, shaking with the force of the blow. "Just stop. There's no reason for this."

I bolted into motion, sprinting toward them.

"Freaks aren't allowed in this mall." Bobby straightened. "Either go home now, or I'll send all of you home in body bags."

I was just about to reach them when Clarik flew past me and barreled into Bobby. The two propelled into Mercedes, who fell backward with a scream. The two boys rolled into a heavy trash can, grunting. Swinging. Fighting.

"My foot," Mercedes cried. "My foot!"

Mall goers scrambled out of the way as Bobby threw a punch. Clarik dodged it and threw one of his own, landing a solid blow to Bobby's nose. Blood instantly poured.

I didn't try to stop them this time; I was too concerned for Mercedes. Her ankle was trapped and twisted between the legs of the table. My mouth dried as she sobbed and grasped at her leg, trying to free herself.

When I attempted to help her, Linnie shoved me backward. I tumbled into Avery, who wrapped her arms around me to steady me. "Leave her alone," Linnie spat out. "You and your friends have done enough!"

"Mercedes," I began, stepping forward again.

"Leave me alone," she said, sobbing. "Just leave me alone. I hate you. I hate you!"

Amid Mercedes's groans and grunts of pain, Erica gently pried her injured ankle from the table legs. "Should we take her to a hospital?" she asked Linnie, frantic worry in the undertones. "What should we do?"

"Yes, take her to the hospital," I said softly. Mercedes's rejection stung in a way I didn't understand. I'd thought we'd come to a truce. I'd thought . . . I'd thought we'd started to like and respect one another. "Her ankle is already turning blue." As I spoke, I saw a security guard hurrying down the escalator.

My focus whipped to the still-raging fight. Clarik had pinned Bobby to the ground and was punching him once, twice. There was such rage in his expression, I blinked, unsure I was seeing correctly. "Clarik! Stop, okay. You have to stop."

He didn't even pause.

"Clarik!"

This time, he faced me. There was blood on his hands and a stream of crimson trickled from his cracked lip. Bobby lay on the ground, moaning.

"Come on." I motioned him over. "Security will be here any second."

His gaze flicked behind me and he jumped to his feet. With a final glance to Mercedes, I grabbed Clarik's hand and took off in a dead run.

chapter thirteen

*How can one's priorities and desires become
so twisted and blurred with only a few
simple life changes?*

We walked back to the school, which wasn't too far, and climbed inside Clarik's car. For a long while, as we meandered along the highway, neither of us spoke. I didn't know what to say, really. I kept seeing Mercedes's tear-stained face in my mind, her eyes glazed with pain.

"Are your hands okay?" I finally asked. They were already swollen and slightly blue. Cars zoomed past us on the road. Even though his air conditioner pelted me at full blast, a bead of sweat trickled between my shoulder blades.

"They're fine."

I pushed one of his books with the toe of my boot. "You punched him pretty hard. More than once."

"He deserved it." He paused and drew in a deep, shuddering hiss. "First Bobby yelled at you, then he pushed Mercedes."

We reached Clarik's house, a small, slightly run-down structure in the heart of an even more run-down neighborhood. He ushered me inside, grabbed two frozen pouches of peas, and lead me to his bedroom. I liked the look of it. A small bed with dark blue covers occupied the far wall and another bed stretched against the nearest (stuffed animals were all over it). A few clothes were strewn on the floor. Posters of women in swimsuits covered one side. Posters of airplanes covered the other. There was a desk, a computer, and lots of equipment I didn't recognize. There was even a bookshelf filled with books. Most were about computers, I noticed.

"This is my side of the room," he explained. Of course, he motioned to the side with swimsuit models. "And the other side is my brother's. We share."

"I didn't know you had a brother."

"He was a surprise."

"Where is he?"

"He's too young for school, so he's usually with my aunt. They're probably grocery shopping or something."

"I'm worried about Mercedes," I blurted, unable to hold the words back any longer. I couldn't get the picture of her pained face out of my mind. "I think she broke her ankle."

Clarik flopped on the bed with a tired sigh. He probably hurt all over. "I thought you hated her."

"I don't," I admitted, pacing. And it was the truth. "Not really. I guess she's kind of grown on me."

"Bobby will think twice before he pushes her again. What a dick."

"I had no idea of his true awfulness until today."

Clarik rolled to his side and pinned me with an odd stare. I don't know what he was looking for in my expression, or if he found what he wanted. I couldn't read him.

I wanted to tell him what happened, I realized, the truth about me and Mercedes. I wanted him to like me enough to believe me. To like me for *me*.

"I—" Wait. Would I be ruining everything? When someone knew your deepest, darkest secrets, they had power over you. They could use the knowledge against you. They could tell the entire school. I drew in a deep breath. Would Clarik laugh in my face? He'd already agreed to help me find Ms. Hamilton's home address, so I didn't have to explain. But . . .

It would be so awesome if he knew. And believed me. And sympathized with me. It would be awesome to hear him tell me I wasn't crazy and that he would like me anyway, game or not. That he would like me, no matter the reality.

Take the risk, my mind beseeched. Trust him. I wasn't nervous around him anymore, and was ready for our date. Did I really want him to take me out, when he didn't truly like me for myself?

I gulped, pursed my lips, then did it. I told him everything. From the time I strode into Hammy's office for my punishment, to the time I woke up in my bed, no needle marks. Clarik sat up in bed, listening attentively. Halfway through my explanation, his brow furrowed. By the time I finished, he was scratching his jaw.

I twisted my hands together. "You think I'm crazy, don't you?"

Expression pensive, he stood. Water dripped from his swollen, red hands as he eased into the chair at the desk. Grimacing, he wiped his hands on his jeans and started typing.

"What are you doing?" I asked, curious and unsure and needing some sort of assurance from him.

"Looking for something."

I paused beside him, staring at the screen. At least he hadn't rejected my explanation right away. He hadn't laughed, either.

"I've heard of Laroque," he admitted. "He's a scientist who wants to revolutionize the state of VR games and teenage 'psychoses.'" Clarik said the last word with a sneer. "He's totally capable of doing something like you described."

My mouth fell open in shock, but relief quickly overshadowed everything else. Clarik knew what had happened to me and he believed me. "How do you know that?"

He didn't answer for a long while. Then, as if it were shameful, he admitted, "At Ms. Hamilton's suggestion, my uncle made me visit with the doctor before letting me move into his house."

"What did Laroque do to you?"

His fingers continued to fly over the keyboard. "He talked with me a bit, then decided I had too much repressed rage to enter a game of my own. I, uh, was constantly in fights at my old school and always getting expelled."

"Don't be mad at me for saying this, okay, but you *do* have a lot of repressed rage."

"I know," he said quietly, distantly. "Back then it was," he shrugged, "I don't know. My dad had just taken off—again— after beating the shit out of my mom. Everywhere I looked I saw his face and just wanted to hurt him."

Oh. I reached out and clasped his shoulder. "I'm sorry."

"When I saw Bobby push Mercedes . . ." He pounded his fist against the desktop, shaking its foundation. "No one should have to fear getting beat up, especially a girl." He took a moment to breathe, then gestured to the computer, effectively ending that line of our conversation. "Look at this. I didn't have any luck with Ms. Hamilton's address, but I was able to find a mention of her."

Excitement sparked inside me as I bent down. My gaze scanned over the article about a man—John Laroque—who'd been fired from the Paranormal Sciences Division of some university in Boston for unethical behavior. "I can't believe Ms. Hamilton put me in the hands of that quack," I said.

"Seems he didn't quite learn his lesson about unethical behavior." Clarik's chair swiveled as he faced me. "Did you see the part where they mention his intention to write a book about his experiments with the help of 'Donna Hamilton'?"

"That woman!" I pounded the top of his chair. "She has to show up sometime. And if not, well, I have those papers I stole from her office." Lord, the papers! I had forgotten about them. I'd stuffed them in my locker before heading off to class. "Maybe I'll find a clue or something."

The long length of his eyelashes swept down, casting shadows over his cheeks as he gazed at his hands. "What if—what if you go back and don't remember that you . . . like me?"

I gulped, backed up a step, another and another until I hit the edge of the bed. My knees collapsed and I plopped onto the mattress. That prospect scared me, but in a different way than he assumed. I'd remember that I liked him. The danger was that *he* wouldn't remember *me.*

What would I do if he looked at me like a stranger?

He had propped his elbows on his knees and was watching me, I realized. Watching my lips. Waiting for an answer? Or . . . wanting something more? My face flushed, heat spreading from my forehead to my collarbone. His eyelids raised, looking heavy and oh so sexy. I gulped again.

I hadn't expected to find anything in this new reality that I would like. But I did. I had. And, well, I didn't want to give him up. Or the other things I'd grown to appreciate.

Without a word, Clarik stood and closed the small distance between us. He knelt in front of me and splayed his hands over my knees. I'd changed into a skirt, and his bare skin touched my bare skin. A shiver danced through me at the first hint of contact.

"My uncle's not here," he said huskily. We were nose-to-nose, and our breath mingled together. "Neither is my aunt or my brother."

"I'm glad," I said on a wispy catch of breath. My heart skipped a beat.

"I want to kiss you."

"I'm not stopping you." I wanted to kiss him. Badly. Wanted, *needed* to feel the press of his lips, to experience my first kiss. With him. Only him.

"You're sure?"

"Yes." I leaned down.

He lifted and met me halfway. Our lips pressed together gently, soft and experimental. The warm scent of him filled my nose. Then his tongue flicked out and hesitantly sought entrance into my mouth. I opened for him, welcoming him inside.

Our tongues brushed once, twice. He tasted hot and oh so sweet, like fire and Strawberry Julius. The effects of the kiss ricocheted through my entire body, licking at my blood, sizzling me from inside out. On and on we tasted each other.

A kiss was like entering the gates of heaven, Linnie had once told me. She was right.

"Jade," he whispered.

"Clarik."

"I don't want to stop."

"I don't want you to stop, either."

"But I have to." There was regret in his tone. And longing. And need. And pain.

The thought of his mouth pulling away from mine had me moaning in disappointment. "Just . . . a little . . . more."

"Okay. You talked me into it." His tongue thrust deep into my mouth. Hard. Delicious.

My arms slid up his chest and tangled in his hair. The strands were silky, and I could have stayed exactly where I was for . . . eternity. His hand trailed up my legs and anchored onto my lower back. He tugged me forward, until there was nothing but a whisper separating us.

I knew I'd write stories about this moment for years to come. The kiss, well, it somehow made up for every time I'd been called a freak, made up for every boy who'd ever picked Mercedes over me. Made up for the horror I'd endured at the change in my realities.

He drew his hands up, up, and around, then cupped my cheeks. Slowly, with regret, he ended the kiss. I gazed up at him through heavy eyes, panting a little. His lips were wet, swollen, and a darker shade of pink than before.

"I don't think I want you to go back," he said roughly. "I like *this* reality."

Me too. God, me too. In that moment, I liked it so very much. I wanted to stay forever.

The sound of a car door slamming jolted us both and we jumped apart guiltily. I stood. Clarik popped up, too, and strode to the window. He parted the blinds. "My aunt and brother," he said. "Do you want to stay for dinner?"

"No," I said with regret. "I need to get home."

"I'll drive you."

I cleared my throat, trying to fight the drugging effects of his kiss. Trying to act as if my knees weren't about to collapse. "Will you stop by the school first, so I can get my stuff?"

"Won't the building be locked?"

"No. It stays open for the jocks at practice." We didn't move toward the car, though. He linked our fingers together and we stood in place, simply looking at each other. No, I didn't want to give this up.

What the hell was I going to do?

chapter fourteen

If I could go back in time and change aspects of my life, would I still be the girl I am today? Would I be better? Worse? It's odd to think that if one tiny thing were different, I'd be different.

That evening, I locked myself in my room despite my dad's desire for a heart-to-heart. He then invited me to have dinner with Susan, Mercedes, and Lara (the younger sister), all of whom he had invited over.

I wanted to see them.

I was still worried about Mercedes. I'd tried to call her. No answer. She was never far from my mind, though, as I leafed through the papers I'd stolen from Ms. Hamilton's office.

Among those were the papers with nothing but gibberish and the file I'd taken on Clarik.

He hadn't lied. His mom had signed custody of him over to her brother, his uncle. She'd left him and his young brother—in every sense of the word—and never looked back. His dad was in jail for assault and battery, and Clarik himself had been arrested and even placed in a home for violent teens.

He had one more chance to get his life together and Hell High was it. He'd almost blown that today by fighting Bobby. He *might* have blown it, if anyone ratted him out.

He might be a fighter, but with me he was nothing but a . . . boyfriend. How odd it was to think that word in conjunction to myself. But he'd kissed me. Oh, had he kissed me (with tongue!). I sighed dreamily and fell back on my carpet, splaying myself out. I smiled up at the ceiling. Clarik. I could say his name a thousand times and it wouldn't be enough.

"Jade?" my dad said, knocking on my door.

Good-bye dreamy remembrance. I frowned. "Yeah?"

"Susan called and canceled. Mercedes broke her ankle."

I jolted to my feet and pounded to the door, then quickly unlatched the lock and swung the door open. "Did she say anything else? How's Mercedes doing?"

"She was at the mall, got into a fight, and broke her ankle. Susan's been at the emergency room with her and they just got her home. Poor thing is in a cast."

My cheeks colored with guilt. "Should we, maybe, go over there and see how she's doing? Maybe we should send her flowers."

"Yes on the flowers, no on the visit." He shook his head and traced a finger along my cheekbone. "Mercedes is sleeping and Susan doesn't want to disturb her."

I nodded in understanding.

My dad's hand fell to his side and his expression acquired a sad, almost curious cast. Uh-oh. Trouble for sure. "That's what happens when teenagers lead such a nonconformed life, I guess."

Nonconformed? Mercedes? Please. Her biggest crime was snobbery. "There's nothing wrong with expressing one's individuality, Dad. That doesn't make the person evil or make them deserving of bad things." How many times would I have to give this speech?

He said nothing, but his chin canted to the side and he regarded me as if I'd spoken a foreign language. Hated to break it to him, but I'd failed Spanish.

"I truly doubt you'd like the world if everyone looked the same, talked the same, and acted the same." On a tangent now, I couldn't have closed my mouth if God himself reached down and clamped my lips shut. "What if Susan looked just like every other woman in the world? Would she still be special to you?"

"Well . . ."

"I didn't think so."

He crossed his arms over his chest and leaned against the doorframe. "Sweetie, Mercedes is wild."

Is that what he'd thought of me? Before the switch, I mean? Had he seen me as a wild nonconformist who caused trouble and basically deserved any hard times that came my way? "Think about what I said, okay? Think about how bland and unhappy the world would be without people like me— uh, Mercedes—who add spice." With nothing more to say, I shut the door in his stunned face.

Mercedes missed the next day of school. And the next. I called her several times each evening, but she ignored me. Once Linnie had answered her phone and told me where I could rot for eternity. I'd heard Mercedes laughing in the background.

She'd obviously begun to like this reality, as well—with *my* friends, who weren't really my friends anymore. It was Avery who called me every night and talked about boys and clothes. Avery who sought my advice and helped me with homework. She didn't care that I didn't want to date her brother; she liked me no matter what.

And I liked her.

There. I had admitted it without any hint of guilt or embarrassment. I liked her. I did.

On the third day, the vice principal announced that poor, sick Ms. Hamilton (sick in the head, was my diagnosis) would be out another week and that he was going ahead with all student activities—including class elections. Which meant . . .

"You're so going to win," Avery said after first period. She linked our arms and we skipped down the hall. "Don't be nervous. You look amazing."

"I'm not nervous."

Cheesy joined us, chatting about my magnificence, as well. "You've never looked better, and you'll be the best president ever! You can talk to Hammy about finally putting together a black magic class."

I looked the same as always in my jeans and a fringed black top. Nothing special about my outfit. Nothing different about my hair or makeup. But today I felt different. Stronger. More assured. And it was a good feeling. Maybe I'd finally found my place in the world.

"There's no way you can lose," Cheesy continued. "Everyone adores you. Just *adores* you."

Where was Clarik? I wondered. I hadn't caught sight of him today. Hadn't caught sight of him all week, actually. He'd missed several days—and I'd missed *him*. He'd called me a few times, but that wasn't the same as seeing him. Especially when, early this morning, I'd been struck by a horrible thought that refused to leave me. What if I was pulled from the game? No warning, no finding Ms. Hamilton or Dr. Laroque or the computers. Just *boom!* Here one moment, gone the next.

What then?

I wasn't ready to leave. I wanted to spend more time with Clarik, to kiss him some more. I wanted to become class president and show my former friends and Mercedes that I was someone important. That other people adored me.

"—and I've been waiting for this all year, Madam President," Avery was saying.

"I bet Bobby has the first formal request," Cheesy said. "He'll want you to petition the school board for a skankier dress code for the girls."

"How *is* Bobby?" I asked Avery. He, too, had missed school this week.

She waved her hand in dismissal. "He has a black eye and a busted nose, but it's no more than he deserves for bullying you."

I noticed she said nothing about his bullying Mercedes, and that sparked a little stirring of irritation inside me. "Did he come to school today?"

"Yeah, he's around here somewhere." Her face scrunched with concern, creasing worry lines in her forehead. "Clarik's not going to fight him again, is he?"

"No." I hoped not, at least. I might like the image of Bobby moaning and groaning in a fetal ball of pain, but I didn't want Clarik in trouble.

Avery breathed a sigh of relief. "Thank God. Clarik's quite . . . fierce, isn't he?"

"He's a total he-man," Cheesy said on a dreamy sigh, "and that's what makes him so freaking hot. Jade is so lucky."

We strolled the rest of the way down the hall, arm in arm. Everyone gazed at the three of us with admiration and awe in their eyes. Several kids stopped and waved at us. A few even vied for our attention. Avery and Cheesy ate it up, and I admit, I did, too. There was a new strut to my walk, confidence in my every step.

"Hey, Jade," someone said.

"Hey," I replied.

"Looking good." Someone else.

"Thanks." I smiled.

Linnie strode past me, but didn't say anything. Didn't even look at me. I held my chin high, not speaking to her, either. From best friends, to *this*. It was sad. Nothing I could do about it now. And I found that didn't bother me anymore.

"Next up is homecoming queen, isn't it?" I asked Avery, a little excited by the prospect.

"Yep. Then prom queen, then Miss Haloway. You'll be the first girl to win all three in the school's history." Avery stretched out her arm and pointed. "Look." Her voice dropped to a half-excited, half-fearful whisper. "There's Clarik."

My heart skipped a beat as I dragged my gaze through the hallway, searching for him. There! At the end of the hall. When our eyes collided, he stopped walking. I stopped walking. He grinned slowly. I grinned slowly. He began striding toward me and I kicked into motion, careful not to skip. Avery and Cheesy stayed beside me, eager to hear our conversation, I guess.

"Hey," Clarik said, his eyes only for me.

"Hey, yourself," I said.

"I heard about the election. Are you nervous?"

"Not really." I hadn't signed up for it, had once thought I'd hate it, but I wanted to win now. I *would* win. Everyone would be impressed. I'd be set apart, the absolute leader of this school.

Avery sighed and said, "There's Mercedes. She looks so . . . sad. I don't know why, but that makes *me* sad." The instant she realized she'd spoken, her cheeks colored with mortification. "I can't believe I said that out loud. I must be on drugs. Who cares about that freak, right?"

I stared at Avery hard, trying to read her. Okay. What had just happened? She shouldn't like Mercedes, not even a little. Were her true feelings seeping through? Was the game weakening? Or did it reprogram itself with our actions?

Had this . . . softening happened with *my* former friends?

Mercedes didn't glance in our direction as she crutched past us. Her features were pale and pinched. Erica strode beside her, carrying her books. She leveled me with a glance and a frown, but there was more curiosity in that frown than heat.

I felt a wave of panic that I'd be taken from this reality, and all that I'd gained would be lost without warning. I forced myself to stay calm.

"It's okay," I said to Avery. "We all go a little crazy sometimes."

"Come on." Clarik clasped my hand. "Let's get you to the assembly."

"Avery, Cheesy," I said, "will you go ahead and save us seats?"

"Sure," they replied in unison, laughed, then bounded off with happy grins.

Clarik winked at me, a teasing sparkle in his blue eyes. "Needed some alone time with me, huh?"

"Clarik," I said, but I looked up at him and the rest of my words faltered. I'm not sure what I had wanted to say anyway. After the thing with Avery, then with Erica, I did have a sudden need to have Clarik to myself, to hold onto him so I wouldn't lose him. "Did you, uh, find anything else on Ms. Hamilton?"

He shook his head. "No. It's like she deleted all of her information."

"Maybe she *did*."

Someone suddenly rammed into him from the side, propelling him backward. I gasped, tugged along with him. He straightened and whipped around. Bobby—whose face was cut and bruised, I noticed with satisfaction—had gathered a large group of his friends. They were lined up beside him like a testosterone parade.

My stomach knotted with dread. Not now, I silently moaned. Not with Clarik so close to expulsion. "What are you doing, Bobby?" I said, trying my best to sound stern, like a teacher. Or Ms. Hamilton. That woman could frighten the devil.

Bobby's attention didn't waver from Clarik. "I just want to

prove your *boyfriend*"—he sneered the word—"isn't as tough as he thinks he is."

Scowling, I anchored one fist on my hip and glared up at him. "So you have your friends gang up on him? All that proves is how weak *you* are. Put your big boy panties on, Bobby, and act somewhat intelligent."

Clarik stepped in front of me, blocking me with his body. "Go to the assembly, Jade. You don't need to stay for this."

"Yeah, it's gonna be a bloodbath," Bobby said with a relishing grin.

"I'm not leaving," I said bravely. Inside, I admit, I shook and teetered back and forth between decisions. Should I go get help? Should I scream? Should I, maybe, flirt with Bobby to calm him down? What should I do, what should I do?

"Fight," I heard the kids in the hall begin to chant. "Fight! Fight! Fight!"

People were gathering around, assembly forgotten, ready to watch the slaughter. See the carnage. "Someone go get—"

"No," Clarik said, cutting me off. "Bobby didn't learn his lesson about picking on people smaller than him, so I'm going to make sure he does this time."

"Go get help," I commanded the girl next to me.

"Do it and you'll regret it," Bobby snapped.

She froze in place. What should I do? I wondered again, a little more desperately.

"You want a piece of me," Clarik said, stepping forward, "you come and get it."

Bobby, too, stepped forward. His friends flanked his sides.

Just then a girl came rushing forward, the vice principal in tow. "Stop!" he called. "Stop. Right. Now!"

A relieved breath gushed from me as kids quieted. Just like that, the potential for a fight ended and disaster was slimly avoided.

Mr. Bradford stepped in the middle of the boys, panting, glaring at Clarik. "Clarik Spanger, gather your belongings and march straight into my office. I knew you'd be trouble the first day I laid eyes on you. You should never have been allowed to enter these halls, and I'll make sure you aren't allowed to come back."

"But Mr. Bradford," I said, "Clarik didn't—"

"Thanks for your help, Mr. Bradford," Bobby said, fighting an evil grin. "I wasn't sure what to do when Clarik threatened me."

"But—"

Clarik banged his fist against a locker. "Figures I'd get the blame." He spun around and stalked away, never glancing backward.

chapter fifteen

My mom used to tell me anything was possible. I wish that were true, but I haven't been able to bring her back, and I haven't been able to gain acceptance for who I am. People are the most difficult thing in the world to change.

I tried to run after Clarik, but Mr. Bradford stopped me by jumping into my path and wagging a finger in my face. "Where do you think you're going, young lady? You have an assembly to attend, and your attendance is mandatory. Ms. Hamilton called me from her sick bed, demanding that I make sure you were there."

I stilled. "You talked to her? What else did she say?"

"Uh, uh, uh. No questions."

My teeth ground together. So. Ms. Hamilton *was* in this reality. She was avoiding Mercedes and me, as we'd suspected, and wasn't just a name here. "Clarik was not at fault, you know."

"Girls have been defending bad boys for centuries, Miss Leigh." With a sweep of his arm, he motioned me in front of him. "Now walk."

On the way to the auditorium, I explained what really happened. Mr. Bradford nodded in all the right places, but refused to change his mind about who was to blame. I didn't understand that. All the other teachers did what I told them to do. Had he been programmed to resist me?

"He's a menace, Jade, and destined for prison. I'm surprised your father allows you to hang out with someone like Clarik Spanger. He should fear for your life."

"Mr. Bradford—"

"No, not another word from you."

Grrr. We had reached the seats. He ushered me to the front row, patted my shoulder, and strolled onto the stage. He then launched into a speech about honor and integrity and nonviolent ways of expressing oneself.

Avery sat beside me. She reached over and squeezed my hand. "What happened?"

"Everything I didn't want to happen," I muttered. What was I going to do? Clarik didn't deserve to be kicked out of school. He had rough edges, yes, but he protected those weaker than himself. Weren't people supposed to be commended for that?

God, what a nightmare! Things had seemed so promising only a half hour ago. I had a new group of friends. I was popular and adored, with a boyfriend who really, really liked me. Now . . . I had the friends, I was still popular, was still adored, but the boyfriend who liked me might be taken away and there was nothing my new friends or popularity could do to stop that from happening.

Mr. Bradford's prejudice against Clarik was like Mr. Parton's prejudice had been against me. Unfounded. Unneeded. Unwelcome.

Stupid.

Why were people like that? Why was there so much hate?

"There's no need for further delay. The new senior class president is . . ." Mr. Bradford grinned and pushed his glasses high on his nose. "This is no surprise. I think you'll all be delighted." He gave a dramatic pause.

"Tell us," someone shouted from the crowd.

Chuckles circled the room.

"Give a round of applause for . . . Jade Leigh!" Mr. Bradford clapped. "She's your new class president. This will surely prove to be a stupendous year!"

Cheers and whistles erupted. Applause abounded. I'd been gazing at my hands, but at the sound of my name, my head popped up. Gulping, I looked around. Everyone watched me expectantly.

"Get up there, silly," Avery said with a wide grin. "You won. You won!"

I'd wanted this to happen, right? At that moment, I

couldn't remember. I stood, my legs shaky, and trudged up the platform steps. If the choir had been here, I know they would have burst into song.

I finally stood at the podium and stared out at the still-cheering crowd. Bright lights enveloped me, but I could make out a few faces. I even—yes! I could see Clarik standing in the back, leaning against one of the walls. He grinned at me encouragingly, had probably sneaked in here to watch me.

"I knew you'd be trouble," Mr. Bradford had told him. The same words Mr. Parton had once said to me.

"She's wild," my dad had said about the fake Mercedes, meaning *I* was the wild one in his eyes.

"Woohoo!" someone called.

"You rock, Jade!"

"Thanks," I said into the microphone. My voice echoed in my ears and I cringed. "Thank you everyone for voting for me." *They didn't vote for you, though, did they?*

"Go, Jade, go!"

"I'll try to . . ." What? What should I say? "I'll try to be a good pres . . . ident." The moment I spoke, my eyes locked with Mercedes. She looked jealous and miserable and everything inside me froze. The utter wrongness of my words echoed in my ears, drowning out all the other voices. My lips pressed together, my hands clenched the podium.

That's all it took, that one heartbeat of suspended time, and I knew. *Knew.*

This was wrong. Somehow, along the way, I'd begun losing my true self. If not for the game, these students would consider me a freak. Unworthy. They would hate me, put me down.

What was I doing, accepting this position? What the hell was I doing?

I wanted it for all the wrong reasons. To prove myself? Yes. But I shouldn't need to win a popularity contest to do that. To put Linnie, Erica, Robb, and Mercedes in their perceived places because they hated me? Undoubtedly. But the same thing had been done to me over and over again, people putting me in my "place." How could I do that to someone else? Someone I was supposed to love?

I gazed out, taking in the expectant faces. The girl you voted for isn't me, I thought. Not really. Not the *real* me. I shouldn't be here. This victory belonged to someone else, to *her*. The *real* her.

The hatred had to stop.

In the next instant, something inside me snapped. Complacence, maybe. Acceptance, surely. I couldn't let this go on. Whether I got back to my reality or not, things had to change. "Mercedes Turner, come up here, please," I said. My voice didn't waver, though I was shaking inside.

A collective gasp rang out.

Mercedes violently shook her head no.

"I don't deserve this honor," I said. "You do. Come up here. Please."

"Jade," she growled. She looked around. "Stop."

"No. We need to end the war between us once and for all. We need to end the war between Goths and Barbies."

"Jade . . ."

"Please."

There was dead silence as she slowly stood and hobbled to the dais. A few of the more disruptive students threw paper wads at her. Agonizing seconds ticked by, until finally, she stood beside me. She placed her hand over the microphone and whispered fiercely, "I have to tell you something."

"And I have to tell the school something." I pried away her hand and faced the crowd. I had to do this; it needed to be done, and had for a long time. "The Barbies are not freaks, and we should be ashamed of ourselves—"

"Shut up, Jade. You're just going—"

"—for treating them—"

"—to make everything—"

"—that way."

"—worse for me."

"They might dress differently, but that doesn't make them less than we are. We all have hopes and dreams, thoughts and feelings."

"Clarik is working for Ms. Hamilton," Mercedes blurted out.

"What?" I shouted, facing her.

"He's working for Ms. Hamilton." Her voice echoed throughout the stadium. "I wasn't going to tell you, but you wouldn't shut up! Everyone already calls me a freak. I don't need them calling me Jade Leigh's charity project, too. You're sweet to do this, you are. I admit that. But I can fight my own battles."

My vision went black and red for a moment and my breath snagged in my throat. "You're lying about Clarik," I said quietly. "He's not."

Throughout the crowd, whispers of "What are they talking about?" trickled to us, quiet at first, but quickly growing in volume.

"I wouldn't lie about something like that. He's part of the game. Hammy's been having him watch us and report to her all along. I found her notes. They were in the papers I photographed in her office."

"What's going on, girls?" Mr. Bradford demanded.

"Jade," Clarik called from the crowd. "Jade, listen to me. Let me explain."

The second time he spoke my name, he sounded closer to me. He must be racing toward me, I thought, but I couldn't tell because my eyes were so watery. I turned and ran. I pounded out of the side door in the auditorium, out of the building.

He caught up with me in the parking lot and latched onto my arm, grinding me to a halt. "Let me explain," he said, panting.

"Is it true?" I demanded, facing him. I wiped at my eyes angrily.

He was pale and frowning. "Yes." I attempted to run

again, but he grabbed on to my shoulders and held me in place. "I was supposed to take you out that first day and show you that everyone was Goth. I did that. I reported in. Since then I've told her little things, but not everything. I couldn't. I didn't want to betray you."

"That's funny, because you *did* betray me." I brushed off his hold, but didn't try to escape. How could I have been so stupid to think a boy like him would actually want me? "Everything you said to me has been a lie. You're part of the game. You said they didn't put you in the game!"

"I never lied, Jade. Never. I said they didn't put me in my own game. They put me in *yours*. I was going to tell you. I planned to tell you tonight, actually."

"Why would you do this?" I closed my eyes, blocking out his face for the flash of time I needed to get myself under control. "Just tell me why."

He looked tortured. "Ms. Hamilton wasn't going to allow me in this school, and if she wouldn't let me in I'd be sent away and put in a home. I didn't know you at the time, so I said yes. I regretted it the moment I met you. You have to believe me."

"Do you know where she's staying then? Did you lie about that?"

"No. We met at the lab. I swear to you."

That doused some of my anger, but none of my hurt. "You talked about wanting me to stay here so you wouldn't forget me. You're part of the game. You won't forget. You knew that. Just more of your lies, I guess."

"No." He shook his head, a desperate gleam in his eyes. "I said I didn't want to go back to the other reality. I was afraid you'd find out what I'd done and stop liking me."

"You were right." I laughed bitterly and turned away from him.

"I know how to help you get back," he rushed out. "I think I can duplicate the game, just in reverse. When the doctor hooked me up, I watched him. I just need the codes. If we can find them, I can take us back."

I stopped mid-step, then slowly turned toward him. At that moment, I didn't like him, but just then I would have worked with the devil to get home. "I stole some papers from Ms. Hamilton's office. There was a bunch of numbers and stuff on them."

He brightened. "That's it! That's what I need."

I arched a brow, watching his expression. "And if you're kicked out of school for helping me return?"

"I'll deal with it," he said, determined though some of the light dimmed. "I *will* make this up to you. I didn't lie about liking you, Jade. I like you. A lot. You're sweet and caring and you make me laugh."

I didn't respond to his declaration. I couldn't. I felt too raw, too exposed. "Take me home," I said softly, "and I'll give you the papers."

chapter sixteen

How do the people in heaven see through the masses and find their loved ones? For the life of me, I can't think of an answer. And more than anything, I want my mom to see me, to watch over me.

the next morning, I dressed like a Barbie clone. That's right. You didn't misunderstand. A Barbie clone. I wore my mom's favorite Sunday dress, a flowing ivory number with lace and pink bows. I'd had to dig through a box of her old things, and had cried. Afterward, I even washed the dye from my hair and now the dark blond tresses cascaded down my shoulders.

I felt weird, but strangely *right*.

I was Jade Leigh, pure and simple. I would not conform,

would not be part of a crowd that hated everything different. Would not be what everyone thought I should be. I would simply be *me,* with all my faults, all my shortcomings.

Let the world call me a freak. I didn't care. Other people didn't have to live with the consequences of *my* actions. Other people did not determine the amount of happiness I would have. I did that. And I would be happy with myself. I would be happy with my life, no matter what names others called me.

My dad drove me to school with only a muttered, "Costume party?" He continually cast shocked glances in my direction. "If you're doing this to prove a point—"

"I'm not. I'm doing it for *me.*"

"I love you for who you are, Jade," he said, and there was truth in his voice. "No matter how you dress. You know that, don't you?"

I looked over at him and slowly smiled. "I do now."

Once we reached the building, I kissed his cheek and exited the car with my head high and my shoulders squared. I strolled into Haloway High to the sounds of shocked gasps. My chin never lowered.

"Is that Jade Leigh?"

"No way."

"Jade? Is that you?"

"Why is she dressed like a freak?"

"She likes them. Hello, remember the assembly?"

"She's committing total social suicide," someone muttered.

"Why does there have to be different *Goths* and *Barbies*?" I asked no one in particular. "Why can't there just be people?"

Avery, Cheesy, Michelle, and Bobby stood in front of the lockers and stared at me, slack-jawed. They didn't understand what I was doing. Unfortunately they might never understand. The hate had to stop, I thought again, and I was now in a position to help do that.

I might never be in this position again.

"I'll drive you home," Avery said, stepping toward me. She gazed around to see who was watching. "You can change."

"I don't want to change."

"But . . . but . . ." she floundered.

"You either like me for who I am no matter how I'm dressed, or you don't like me at all." With that, I strolled to class.

Mrs. Collins was as shocked as the students. She stumbled over her lesson so many times I lost count. She just couldn't tear her gaze away from me. Shocked was good, though. A good shock would hold their attention and have them talking about it for days afterward. And maybe, when they talked about it, they would begin to see how silly we'd all been.

Midway through class, the door burst open. The scene was eerily familiar, like a flashback to my first day inside the game. I experienced a jolt this time, too, and straightened in my chair.

Mercedes crutched swiftly inside. "I'm sorry for what I

said to you yesterday," she rushed out her gaze immediately finding mine. "but he did it." Her gaze landed on me and she gasped. "Why are you dressed like that? You look so weird! It doesn't matter," she said without a breath. "Clarik really did it. I didn't believe him at first, but he convinced me!"

Immediately I stood. "When did you talk to him?"

"A few minutes ago." If she hadn't been wearing a cast, she would have been jumping up and down with excitement. "I don't know how he got the number, but he called my Side-kick. I ignored him, so he e-mailed me. He gave me an address for a place downtown and said to meet him there. Right now! He's going to send us home, Jade. We can go home!"

"This is unacceptable, Miss—"

I didn't hear the rest of Mrs. Collins's speech. I was already tugging Mercedes from the room. She hopped behind me as fast as she could. Erica, Linnie, and Robb were waiting in the hallway. I stopped in surprise.

"What's going on?" I asked.

"Mercedes explained what's been going on," Erica said. "I'm not sure I believe her—sorry, Sades, but you do sound crazy insane—but I just wanted to say I'm sorry for the way I treated you. Your speech yesterday was . . . nice."

"Ditto," said Linnie.

"Yeah, ditto," said Robb. His hands were in his pockets and he rocked on his heels.

In that moment, I wanted to hug them and never let go. How could I have forgotten how wonderful they were?

"Go back to class, guys," Mercedes said, grinning. "Jade and I can take it from here."

They nodded and trekked off, leaving Mercedes and me alone in the hall. We didn't waste any more time. We headed for the parking lot, eager to reach Clarik and end this universe switch once and for all.

"We have to get my papers," she told me. With every moment that passed, her excitement intensified. "Clarik already has yours but said he needs mine to hopefully complete the equation, then we're home free! I almost can't believe it."

"Where are the papers?" There was a spring in my step, too, and I couldn't wipe away my grin. I never would have imagined today would have turned out to be so sweet.

"They're at my house. Remember, I snapped pictures of them and printed them off my computer."

"Right." We stood outside, hundreds of cars lined up in front of us. "Where's your car?"

"Uh, hello. Broken ankle." She waved her hand down her leg. "My—your—*our* friends have been bringing me to school. We'll have to take your car."

A lead ball dropped into my stomach, draining my enthusiasm, wiping away my smile. "I don't drive, Mercedes." I faced her, silently begging her to understand. "Ever."

She showed no mercy. "Well, you'd better start. Run home and get your car, then come back and pick me up."

"No." I shook my head to better emphasize my words. She had to understand. I couldn't get behind the wheel of a car. I just couldn't.

"You're wasting time, you big baby. Go get your car."

"We'll call a cab," I said desperately.

She puffed out a breath, lifting several strands of hair from her forehead. "Do you have the time or the money? Go. Start running."

"No." I stomped my foot. I would not cave on this issue.

"Start running, Jade Leigh, or I'll tell my mom I think she should marry your dad!"

I ran.

My blood chilled as I sprinted to my house. The seemingly endless mile gifted me with burning lungs and throbbing muscles. Panting, I grabbed my car keys (which I kept in my desk drawer) and even got inside the car and managed to start it. It was a year old but it had been used so little, it still smelled like a brand-new car.

"I can do this." Breath wheezed from my throat. "I can." I gripped the wheel so tight my knuckles turned white. What if someone slammed into me? What if— "Don't think that way. Just drive."

Tentatively I placed the car in reverse, but I jabbed the brakes the moment it moved. Was that the squeal of tires I heard? Dear God. I wiped the sweat from my brow.

"You're dressed like a Barbie. For God's sake, you can do anything."

I eased off the brakes. My breath emerged shallow and choppy. Ohmygod. Okay. Moving. It was moving. Ohmygod. Tears streamed down my cheeks as images of my mom tried to invade my mind.

The car jerked to a stop. I gulped, straightened my shoulders. "I'm brave," I said with false confidence. "I can do anything, just like my mom once told me."

My foot eased off the brake, and the car once again inched into motion. Slowly I passed one car (without having a panic attack), then two (without having a panic attack). I kept a steady pace, and finally, at long last, made the two-minute drive in fifteen.

Mercedes opened the passenger-side door. "I did it," I told her. "I really did it!"

"Nice of you to come," she said dryly. "I'm thinking we *should* have called a cab. Do you know how many times security passed me?"

"Shut up and get in." I issued the command with a smile. For the first time in two years, I'd battled my fear and won. I'd driven!

Mercedes had trouble with her crutches, so she tossed them on the ground.

Shaking, I eased/stopped/eased the car into motion. Yes, I'd beaten the fear. That didn't mean I felt no terror at all.

"When we get back, I'm throwing a party." Mercedes clapped her hands with relish. "It will be the biggest party Haloway has ever seen." She paused, then added hesitantly, "You'll come, won't you? Erica, Linnie, and Robb will be invited, too."

I blinked at her. "Are you sure you want to do that?"

"Yes. I wouldn't have made it through this without you guys. They're not so bad, your friends."

Wow. "Yes. I'd love to come." Surprisingly I managed to bypass security without hassle and safely reach her house. She gave me her house key, told me where the papers were, and I sprinted inside and gathered them up. Thankfully no one was home.

We were soon on our way downtown.

"You drive like my grandma," Mercedes said on a sigh.

"Then your granny is a wicked excellent driver."

"Speed up."

"Shut up!"

Cars honked and swerved around us.

"Look," Mercedes said, her tone suddenly serious, picking up our heart-to-heart as if it had never stopped. "Since we've got time"—she cast a pointed glance to the speedometer—"I might as well apologize for what I said about your mom the day after her funeral. My dad had just left and I saw the way yours did everything he could to comfort you. Plus, that's when our parents started dating, and I . . ."

"I understand," I said truthfully. I might have reacted the same way, had the situation been reversed. I'd envied her relationship with her mom. Very much. I'd wanted to lash out at her every time I saw them together.

Thankfully, the conversation helped distract me. By the time we reached the building and parked next to Clarik's car—the only other car in the lot—I wasn't shaking quite so badly. I still wanted to throw up and nearly collapsed when I exited the car.

For a moment, Mercedes and I stood in front of the car, looking at the building. Except for the shuttered windows and lack of graffiti, it looked eerily similar to the one Hammy and Dr. Laroque had used before.

"I don't know about this," Mercedes said, her voice shaky.

"We'll be fine." Would we really? I gulped. "Come on." I forced myself to walk forward.

She hobbled behind me. Before either of us could clasp the knob, the door swung open. Clarik stood in the entrance. My heart flip-flopped. In that instant, as I looked up at him, I realized somewhere between yesterday and today I'd lost my anger toward him. He might have lied in the beginning, but he wasn't lying now. He was helping us now.

Deep down, he wasn't a bad guy. He'd done what he'd had to do to keep himself in school, to get his life in order. Honestly, I would have done the same thing. At one point, I might even have sold my own dad's organs on the black market to get home.

"This is the building they used to send me into the game," he said. "They have two labs. One on the outside—the real world. One on the inside—part of the game. I've been to this one several times and it's almost always empty since the doctor and Ms. Hamilton come and go, in and out of the game." He paused. "Are you ready to go home?"

"God, yes," Mercedes said.

With a shaky hand, I gave him the set of papers I'd gathered at Mercedes's house and fought the urge to throw myself in his arms and hold on to the parts of this reality I'd come to like. The game might end soon and everything between us might change. Our social statuses would for *sure* change. Our lives would change. These next few minutes—hours?—might be all we had. If he still liked me, that is.

He leafed through the gibberish and a palpable air of excitement soon seeped from him. "Dr. Laroque used a code, *this* code, to break our molecules apart like paper through a fax machine and transfer us into the game. I spent most of last night figuring out these numbers," he held up the papers, "and now that I have the rest . . ."

I swallowed the lump in my throat.

"Come on." He rushed past a blue curtain and into a sterile-looking room. We followed tentatively. There were two hospital beds, and computers lined every wall. Clarik began typing at the biggest one. "Clamp those wires on you," he said.

I gulped when I saw them, lying so innocently on the bed. They weren't the same color as the ones Dr. Laroque had used on us, but I still remembered what they'd done to me. I gripped them with a shaky hand and began applying them to my ears, my arms, my stomach. Mercedes and Clarik did the same.

None of us spoke.

Afterward, we all just stared at one another. There was fear in Mercedes's eyes—a fear that probably mirrored my own. Clarik, too, no longer looked proud and eager. He looked nervous.

"Are you sure this will work?" Mercedes finally asked.

"No," he answered honestly.

Her mouth fell open on a gasp. "Then why the hell are we even here?"

"You can wait for the good doctor and Ms. Hamilton to take you out, which might be another year or two, or you can take a chance on me." His eyes became two steel beams that bore into us. "Which is it?"

"You," she said without hesitation.

"You," I agreed. I bit the inside of my lip, my nervous system fluttering wildly. My knees were shaking and I could barely stand up. Then Clarik's eyes met mine. A ribbon of calm worked through me.

"I'll see you on the other side," he said softly.

"Clarik," I said. I paused. I'm not sure what I'd wanted to say. Thank you, maybe. I still like you. Possibly. Do you still like me? Definitely. "Yes, I'll see you on the other side."

He turned back to the computer and typed in a few more numbers. He sighed, faced us. "Is everyone ready? One more set of numbers and we're in." His voice became ominous. "There'll be no turning back."

"What about the IV?" Mercedes suddenly shouted. She latched onto Clarik's hand and held on for dear life. "They hooked me to an IV."

"It's not necessary. I don't think," he added, unsure. "They only used the IV to sedate us."

God, my nervousness returned in full force. My heart began drumming so hard I thought my ribs might crack. What if Clarik was wrong? What if the IVs were essential?

"What if we wake up in a new, worse reality?" Mercedes's hands twisted together and her voice trembled. "What if we fail?"

His lips pulled tight and his eyes darkened. "You're just going to have to trust me. I don't know what else to tell you." He paused. "Jade?"

Doubt and hope continued to battle inside me. But I gulped and nodded, squared my shoulders. Putting all of my faith in someone else wasn't easy, but it was better than staying in this world, stuck forever. Besides, by helping us he was risking permanent suspension. The least I could do was believe in him. "I trust you now, Clarik. I do."

His lips slowly inched into a smile. "Thank you. Mercedes?"

She nodded hesitantly.

He turned to the computer, pushed another round of buttons, and in the next instant he was leaning toward me and kissing me. Demanding, claiming. I was so surprised, I didn't respond at first. When I realized that yes, he still liked me, I kissed him back with all the longing inside me.

If this turned out to be our last moment together . . . I wanted to spend it the right way. My arms wound around him, holding tightly as our tongues pushed and intertwined.

All too soon, I felt a familiar vibration working its way through me.

The kiss stopped suddenly. I closed my eyes, drawing in a breath. In. Out. He did the same, and our breath mingled.

"Oh God," Mercedes said.

"Don't let me go," I whispered to Clarik.

I think he said, "Never," but I couldn't be sure. Darkness surrounded me. Claimed me.

chapter seventeen

*Is it destiny that takes us down certain
paths, or ourselves? And if it's ourselves, do
our decisions change our futures daily?*

"Jade?"

I blinked open my tired eyes. God, they burned. I stretched and rolled on to my back, wanting to sleep a thousand more hours. Maybe then I'd feel rested. Maybe not, though. Sleeping forever sounded like a good idea.

"Jade, sweetie. Can you hear me?"

"Dad?" I forced my eyelids to remain open and stared up at him. He hovered over me, concern darkening his features.

"Are you okay? Ms. Hamilton brought you home. She said you passed out on the field trip. I was so worried."

Ms. Hamilton. The field trip. I jolted upright, my forehead banging into his chin. "Ow," we said in unison.

Memories flooded me. The game. Mercedes. Clarik. The computer. Had he been able to make it work and whisk us home? My gaze darted around my room. Same multicolored walls, same dark fairy posters. I glanced over the clothes I wore. Silver shirt and pants. Was that what I'd first worn to the lab?

"Sweetie?"

I almost groaned.

I glanced down at my bare arms and gasped. There was a needle mark above my elbow and bruises on my wrists. Ohmygod, maybe it *had* worked! Not daring to hope, I bounded out of bed. I didn't bother changing. A glance in the mirror showed my hair was black with blue streaks. My hair was black again!

"Slow down, sweetie. You just passed out from fatigue and stress. I don't want that happening again. What's the rush?"

"What time is it?"

"Ten A.M."

I rushed into the bathroom and snatched up my toothbrush. "I have to get to school."

He didn't speak while I brushed my teeth and jerked a comb through my hair. Then, as I tugged on my shoes, he said, "When you were lying so still, Jade, I was afraid that I would never have the chance to tell you how much I love you. I love who you are. I love everything about you."

In that moment, my stomach bottomed out. I froze. Was that something he'd say to me only in the game?

"What's wrong?" he asked. "Are you feeling sick again?"

"I'll be fine." I hoped. Frowning, I forced myself into motion. I grabbed my car keys and sailed out of my room.

"You're *driving*? You don't have a license yet."

"It's less than a mile away, I'll be fine. And it's okay that you're dating Susan Turner, Dad," I shouted over my shoulder.

He had a life and he needed to live it.

I rushed out of the house. Outside—same. Swaying trees, a cool, fragrant breeze. I tried not to let disappointment consume me. Cars lolled on the road, but at least no one honked at me. I drove to school—and I actually went over the speed limit—my heart pounding in my chest all the while: Get there, get there, just get there.

I set off the metal detector, but didn't pause to talk to the guard. "Hey," he shouted.

There were no students in the hallway, so I had a straight run. I ground to a halt in front of the lobby. Posters of Mercedes smiled down on me.

"It worked," I whispered. It really worked. Clarik had done it. We were home!

Mercedes came flying into the building, dressed as haphazardly as me. She wasn't wearing a cast, I noticed with a grin.

"Look," I told her, pointing. "Posters of you!"

Her mouth fell open and she laughed. She even twirled.

"He did it!" She threw herself in my arms. "We're home. We're really home!"

The bell rang and students suddenly poured from their classes. Several people stopped and stared at us, but neither of us cared. We whooped and laughed.

"Mercedes," a familiar voice called. Bobby. He siddled up to her and threw his arm over her shoulder. "You coming over today or what?"

"Hell no." She flicked off his hand and said, "Get lost, asshole."

Shock darkened his expression and his mouth fell open.

"Well, well, well," another voice said.

Dread curdled my stomach as I whipped around. Everything was happening so fast, so wonderfully, I was dizzy with excitement. And dread. Ms. Hamilton stood at the corner, leaning against the wall. Her face was expressionless (as always). Her mousy brown hair was pulled back in a bun and she wore a dark brown suit. "Have fun, girls?"

I bared my teeth in a scowl.

"I see you both survived," she said. A slight twinkle of amusement danced in her eyes. "That was a nice speech, Jade, there at the end."

"You'd better run for your life," I told her, taking a menacing step in her direction.

Mercedes grabbed my arm, holding me back.

Ms. Hamilton grinned. "You owe me a thank-you. We let you into one of the labs without protest, didn't we? We let you come home. Enjoy your day, girls." Without another word, she turned and walked away.

"That's it?" Mercedes gasped. "That's all you have to say to us?"

"I don't want you to punish Clarik for helping us get home," I called.

She paused, but didn't face us. "It was your time to exit, so no worries about Clarik. Besides, I have bigger fish to fry. Starting with this one." She grabbed on to Bobby's arm when he tried to pass her and dragged him toward her office. "I need to talk to you privately, young man," I heard her say. "It's time someone taught you a lesson."

Mercedes and I shared a look before groaning in unison.

"Jade," I heard then.

I swung around, heart hammering at the sound of that familiar, deep voice. Clarik was standing at the end of the hall, a few steps away from me. He was wearing jeans and a T-shirt and looked exactly the same as he had inside the game. Yet, somehow, he'd never looked better.

"We did it," he said. His expression was wary, as if he didn't know what to expect from me.

"Yes. We did." Laughing, I ran to him and threw myself in his arms and kissed him. He locked himself around me and kissed me back.

"I'm so out of here," Mercedes said, flicking her hair over her shoulder. She spotted Avery, squealed, and rushed over to her. "Sweet Jesus, I can't tell you how much I missed you."

"You did promise to take me on a date." I gazed up into Clarik's blue, blue eyes. "Remember?"

"Oh, yeah. I'm just glad you still want to go with me." We kissed again.

Erica, Linnie, and Robb had crowded around me and Clarik, I realized, when I came up for air. They cracked a few jokes at our expense, but I didn't care. They were dressed as Goths and they loved me, and that's all that mattered.

I hugged them all. And if they found my exuberance weird, they didn't say anything. They just hugged me back.

Mercedes and Avery strolled by us, arm in arm. "Hey, Linnie," Mercedes said with a smile. "Hey, Erica. See you around. I'm having a party this weekend and you're all invited. Jade can tell you all about it."

They blinked in surprise, then glanced at me with confusion.

I smiled and shrugged. Oh my Goth, life was good.

Your attitude. Your style.
MTV Books:
Totally your type.

Cruel Summer

First in the
Fast Girls, Hot Boys
series!

Kylie Adams

Life is a popularity contest...and someone is about to lose. In sexy Miami Beach, five friends are wrapping up high school–but one of them won't make it to graduation alive....

The Pursuit of Happiness
Tara Altebrando

Declare your independence.... After her mother dies and her boyfriend cheats on her, Betsy picks up the pieces of her devastated life and finds remarkable strength and unexpected passion.

Life as a Poser

First in the *310* series!

Beth Killian

Sometimes you have to fake it to make it....Eva spends an intoxicating summer in glamorous Hollywood with her famous talent agent aunt in this witty, pop culture-savvy novel, first in a new series.

Plan B
Jenny O'Connell

Plan A didn't know about him....When her movie-star half brother–a total teen heartthrob–comes to town, one very practical girl's plans for graduation and beyond are blown out of the water.

As many as 1 in 3 Americans
have HIV and don't know it.

TAKE CONTROL.
KNOW YOUR STATUS.
GET TESTED.

To learn more about HIV testing,
or get a free guide to HIV and
other sexually transmitted diseases.

www.knowhivaids.org
1-866-344-KNOW